THE WOODLAND SPRITE SERIES

BOOK THREE

THE FARM

The Magic of Dreams and

The Wonder of Wishes

ILLUSTRATED BY NUNO GOMES VIEIRA

FLEUR ROSSDALE

FIRST EDITION

Published by Climate Cooling Initiative Books & Printed by Amazon

ISBN: 978-1-0369-2309-9

To

Riley, Kim and Henry;

Finding wisdom from living

with integrity, in harmony with nature, and finding

beauty, goodness and truth from caring for the

ecosystems we depend upon.

Never giving up hope

while

looking out for each other.

CONTENTS

FOREWORD

Wouter van Dieren

The great explorers and visionaries, the heroes and prophets, the saints and gods – all left behind their strongholds, temples and estates to search for redemption, pacification or the shimmering dream of El Dorado. This quest is etched deep into the soul of humankind: In *The Magic Flute*, Tamino and Pamina must pass through fire and darkness before reaching the Temple of Light. The Queen of the Night must yield before wisdom and harmony can reign.

So it is with the fate of our Earth. The Horsemen of the Apocalypse – famine, poverty, war and death – gallop toward a horizon clouded with despair. Yet, always, just beyond the veil of hopelessness, light returns. Peace follows war. Love follows sorrow. And forgiveness arises like spring after winter's long sleep.

What rekindles that hope is courage of the heart, imagination of the mind and sisterhood with community. These are not abstract ideals. They are real, and they are here – in the hearts of children, in the hands of farmers and in the whispers of the spirits who live in the enchanted forest of our collective memory. These spirits do not exist to entertain. They exist to remind us.

That reminder is the lifeblood of *The Farm*, the third book in Fleur Rossdale's Woodland Sprite Series. Her characters are not only agents of change in a storybook world, but also mirrors of the real work happening around us. Through the eyes of Sky and Anil, we see the fertile dreams of children restoring barren lands. We see communities rising. We see hope not as a flickering candle, but as a wildfire of possibility.

Fleur Rossdale's path has always been as a visionary. During the Covid-19 pandemic, she left behind a distinguished career that propelled British Design onto an international stage to begin writing children's books. Her series, following the adventures of nature sprites, focuses on calming the chaos unleashed by the Four Winds in protest against pollution, born from a sense of urgency and her love of children. In *The Journey*, her second book in the series, she imagined a Changemaker hosting a dinner for thinkers and policymakers in the Pixie Kingdom (her beloved Belgium). This vision was not just fiction, but part of Fleur's vision, which became a reality of her making at fundraising dinners at Maison Frère Orban in rue Ducale.

As a result, we co-founded the Direct Climate Cooling Initiative (DCCI), through inspiration drawn from Sir David King and Professor Stephen Salter, to accelerate ocean-based climate cooling solutions and to reintroduce common sense into climate action. Fleur brought influential players, not just around the table, but also into a shared purpose to cool the planet. The first dinner at Maison Frère Orban on 24 June 2024, planted as a dream in her book, *The Journey,* is now a catalyst for real collaboration and ongoing events.

The stories in *The Woodland Sprite Series* are not merely

allegories. They are blueprints. They give voice to the fears of today's children and offer visions of healing that resonate with scientists, farmers, philanthropists, policymakers and parents.

The Farm brings the story to Africa, where Sky and Anil witness first hand projects inspired by those led by Justdiggit and CEGA, demonstrating the regenerative power of soil, community and purpose. As with any true tale of transformation, the arc bends towards positivity and healing.

Fleur's efforts have reached wider into educational engagement. Through the DCCI School Awards she and her close-knit team invite schools around the world to participate in climate-focused projects, fundraising and accomplishment. Children are performing *Taken by Storm*, her first book in the Woodland Sprite Series, as a play that raises awareness and inspires collective action. Although I am not directly involved with this side of the initiative, I am deeply encouraged by its momentum and reach. Let this book be read not only as a story, but as a seed planted in schools, in villages, in boardrooms and in hearts: For if we listen closely, evil does not vanish with a bang, but with the whispering of the spirit.

WOUTER VAN DIEREN

Club of Rome; World Academy of Arts & Science; Royal Order Oranje Nassau; Vice-Chair Wuppertal Institute for Climate, Environment and Energy (1991- 2005); WWF Global Merit Award (2006); Rachel Carson Gold Medal (2006); Blue Ribbon, Netherlands Parliament (2010); Member NATO Science Committee (1992), Co-Founder Direct Climate Cooling Initiative Brussels (2024); Initiator Amsterdam Climate Forum (ACF) (2025).

AUTHOR'S NOTE

Many of us feel a sense of imbalance and unease due to our disconnection from nature, a detachment that emerged from two centuries of industrial progress, distancing us from the ecosystems that sustain us in an endless race to produce and consume. Not only have we lost sight of what is essential, but see that our actions have left scars, and the weight of those choices is etched in our collective conscience. We now stand at a crossroads: one path leads towards irreversible loss, while the other towards hope and renewal.

The Woodland Sprite Series is a rallying cry for that hope. Through the eyes of fairy sprites – guardians of the natural world – it offers a lens to view challenges that increasingly confront our planet, exploring how humanity's ingenuity and compassion can forge a brighter future. It speaks to a generation eager to reimagine their relationship with the Earth, untangling the complexities of the past two centuries to inspire change in the present.

The Farm, the third book in The Woodland Sprite Series, explores how we grow our food to sustain both people and planet. For decades, industrial agriculture, driven by chemicals, fertilisers and intensive monoculture, has placed enormous strain on the natural world. As global populations rise and the pressure to produce more intensifies, the cracks in the system are becoming harder to ignore. Yet hope lies in the growing movement that seeks to restore rather than deplete: regenerative agriculture. This approach, championed by organisations like the *Soil*

Association, works in harmony with nature to rebuild soil health, increase biodiversity and draw carbon back into the ground. By respecting ecosystems and valuing the life beneath our feet, regenerative farming doesn't just offer an alternative, but a way forward. *The Farm* invites readers to witness the transformative power of community, science and imagination, where pioneering projects and people are already proving that regeneration is not only possible, it's happening.

Readers of *The Farm* are transported into a world where reconnecting with nature is not just a dream, but a necessity. Through the efforts of dedicated individuals and groundbreaking projects, the narrative shows how collaboration and ingenuity can transform even the most strained landscapes into thriving ecosystems. It reminds us that while the challenges are great, the solutions can be greater when we act with courage, creativity and integrity. This tale isn't just a story; it's a call to action for eco-guardians of all ages to be part of the solution, embracing sustainable practices as both a responsibility and a purpose.

Collaboration is at the heart of the mission. The series draws inspiration from real-world pioneers like Robert Rubinstein of TBLI Group, who champions climate-related investments, and Wouter Crul, whose agricultural expertise emphasises that no one can tackle these challenges alone. These changemakers illustrate how collective effort can amplify solutions and scale projects to meet the urgency of the moment and the need for system changes ahead.

The spirit of teamwork extends into classrooms through performances of *Taken by Storm*, the first book in the series, which is brought to life as a stage play performed by schoolchildren around the world. These performances serve as a platform for fundraising and education, supporting the Direct Climate Cooling Initiative (DCCI). This initiative assists communities affected by climate change while supporting projects outlined in the narrative of *The Farm* and celebrated at the DCCI School Awards. Born from the dream seeded into the mind of a powerful and influential changemaker in *The Journey*, the second book in the series, sparks remarkable possibilities for future meetings at Maison Frère Orban in Brussels.

The Woodland Sprite Series is more than a book; it's an invitation to imagine, to act and to join a growing movement of individuals who are willing to make a difference. The time for change is now, and together, we will shape a world where dreams and determination will inevitably lead us back to balance.

'All we have to decide is what to do with the time that is given us.'

J.R.R. Tolkien

Resilience is all about being able to overcome the unexpected.

Sustainability is about survival. The goal of resilience is to thrive.

Jamais Cascio

We are not living an era of change but a change of era.

Jan Rotmans.

FLEUR ROSSDALE

fleur@fleurrossdale.com; www.soot.cloud; www.dcci.earth

PROLOGUE

The gentle winds that once wove harmony through our skies, providing a sense of balance, now roar with unrest – cries reflecting discord in a world that has lost its equilibrium.

Sky and her younger sister Anil, fairy sprites dedicated to protecting nature, hear the desperate calls of the Four Winds in rebellious protest against the direct effects of plastic pollutants and burning fossil fuels upon them, causing the Winds to lose control of the weather. Guided by Titania, Queen of the Fairies, Sky, Anil and teams of nature sprites around the world, embody the imaginative power and determination of children everywhere. Their mission to restore balance to the natural world is an allegory for the vital role young people can play in healing our planet, bringing fresh ideas, compassion, and courage to the urgent work of cooling the Earth and re-establishing biodiversity in the ecosystems that sustain us.

On a mission to make wishes come true, Sky and Anil encounter innovative thinkers, inspiring farmers to nurture the soil, teaching the material world how to rebuild balance. As Sky continues to discover her own strength, she yearns for magic and feels the heavy burden of the impossibility of making wishes come true without it.

Their adventure begins with a call from the sprites of Northumberland to follow their rainbow to Wonderland. Sky and Anil will join their close team of sprites there, with Liam the leprechaun, Kobalos the goblin and Pascal, the pixie prince, sailing by boat, and Robbie the robin redbreast flying cross-country.

Queen Titania, presiding over the Wishing Tree, announces that sprites must be relied upon to make wishes come true for the benefit of nature. Traditional fairies will no longer grant wishes for material possessions, especially when it comes to plastic or anything that harms the natural world.

The dream previously planted into the mind of a changemaker by Sky now becomes a reality, with a dinner in the Pixie Kingdom unfolding new possibilities…

ACKNOWLEDGMENTS

Special thanks to:

Robin & Louella Hanbury-Tenison; Merlin & Lizzie Hanbury-Tenison;

Guy de Selliers and The Duchess of Northumberland

for providing key locations.

Wouter Crul; Robert Rubinstein; Brooke Peterson, Aglaia Ponomareva; Pascal D'Ursel; George & William Robinson; Valeria and Miles Drury for their encouragement and support.

Professor Sir David King; Professor Ian Gadian; Dr. Brian von Herzen; Wouter van Dieren, The Soil Association and Dr. Iain McGilchrist for their inspiration, knowledge and research.

Robert Gerlach, Founder of Klim https://www.klim.eco/en;
Dennis Karpes and Peter Westerveld, Founders of Justdiggit
https://dejongevoedselbosboeren.nl/
and Katja Zweerus, Simon Verboom, Sacha Brons and Wytze Walstra,
founders of de jonge voedselbosboeren
https://dejongevoedselbosboeren.nl/;
Helmy Abouleish, Family Founder of Sekem
https://sekem.com/en/index/; Shadrack Mutembei
https://communitiesevergreening.org/; thousandyeartrust.org, and
Humanity-Insured https://humanityinsured.org/
for projects described in the narrative.

Guy de Selliers; for agreeing the context of his inclusion.
&
Wouter van Dieren; Antoine Laurent & Catherine Turnbull for their mentorship;
Nuno Gomes Vieira for his illustrations.
And to Lisa Davis for her edit.

Enormous thanks goes to
Sponsors and Participants at The DCCI School Awards.

1

A CALL TO WONDERLAND

Like clockwork, Robbie the robin redbreast lands on a branch outside our classroom, preparing to sing a solo. First he tilts his head, waggles his tail feathers and waits for the sun to dip behind the woodland trees of Cabilla. As soon as the sun casts its warm golden glow over the Cornish landscape, Robbie, satisfied that every detail is in perfect harmony, puffs up his chest and begins to sing.

Starting with a tut-tut trill, Robbie builds to a rhythmic, repetitive chirr, his voice cutting through the air as clear as crystal, raising in tempo to a high-pitched whistle. Keen for his message to ride on the breeze, he flutters up to a higher branch, his flawless song ringing out above the woodland. Leaves quiver, amplifying his musical vibrations and passing them through their branches to the Wood Wide Web – an underground network of mycelium threads that will be sure to spread the word.

When the last note fades into the distance, the silent

hush of anticipation signals to our teachers, the Woodland Welfare Workers – better known as The Three Ws – that it is time to close our Nature Sprite School for the summer holidays.

Right on cue, Miss Bracken rings the bell, creating a flurry of activity. Hurriedly, we gather our belongings from lockers and pegs, sprites clambering over each other, opening and slamming desks. Despite the chaos, we manage to fasten our satchels under our wings, filing down the stairs in an orderly procession to shake hands with Mr Woodward, our headmaster.

"Before you go!" Miss Twig calls from the balcony. "These are for you." She scatters tiny envelopes that flutter down like rose petal confetti, catching the light as they drift down over our toadstool play glade. "It's a message from Titania, Queen of the Fairies!"

Darting back and forth, flapping our wings, we catch the envelopes mid-air. I pull out a stiff card bearing the Queen's insignia – a shimmering emblem that glows like captured moonlight. Tracing it with my fingertip, I close my eyes, wrinkle my face, take a deep breath and make a wish: *Please, please, grant me the magic to make wishes come true.* I end by exhaling hard, blowing my words as far as they will carry.

My younger sister, Anil, flies down waving her card to sit beside me. "What does yours say, Sky?" she asks with curiosity.

I glance over her shoulder. "Same as yours. But check out this part!" I lean over and point to a section of the golden script. "'Sprites are called upon to use dreams to inspire wishes in the material world for the natural world to thrive, be it in soil, sea, sky or on land. When a wish to help nature is sent into the Universe from the material world, it's your job as sprites to attract it, catch it and make it come true.'"

Anil claps her hands. "Flickeringfireflies, Sky! That's amazing! It's everything you've ever dreamt of!"

"Don't be too sure, Anil," I frown. "There's no mention of magic. How are we supposed to make wishes come true without it? Tell me that."

Anil shrugs her shoulders. "What about the Wish you caught and read out at the Nature Summit? That one came true, didn't it?"

"Not really," I sigh. "Desert sprites are still suffering from the heat, and the Four Winds are more chaotic than ever." I look down, shaking my head. "The Wish asked sprites to unite nations with rainbows, but it hasn't come to anything. Not as far as I can see."

"But it must have, Sky!" Anil insists, not ready to let it go. "Sprites from two hundred nations held hands, forming rainbows across continents, promising to calm the weather, each united by the love of nature. *You* were up there with them, Sky, shining golden yellow, pledging to do the same."

"Yes," I admit with a glum face. "But, that's the problem. We all want to help, say we will, but don't know what to do. It was simple for countries to say they'd stop burning fossil fuels and put an end to the violent protests of the Four Winds, but it just didn't happen," I say, locking eyes. "Hopeful words and no action, no real changes, and everything going on just as before."

"But the Winds' demonstrations are getting worse! Violent storms, landslides and wildfires that destroy whole communities," Anil exclaims. "How can we be expected to calm the Four Winds and turn things around without using magic? Traditional fairies use it. Why not sprites?"

A thought crosses my mind. "The Wish I read at the summit wasn't made by children in the material world," I say. "It came from sprites of Cabilla, and is possibly why it didn't work."

Anil's eyes widen. "You mean that children's wishes are special?"

"Defo!" I say. "Children have pure, authentic voices. That's where their magic lies, waiting to be discovered."

Anil's face lights up. "Last night, I dreamt of children sitting in a dry field in a faraway land, their voices carried on the wind, but no one heard them. The earth was cracked, desperate for rain. Queen Titania arrived, floating above them, her wand raised, but she didn't wave it. Instead, the words she spoke vanished into mist, leaving tiny shoots rising from the dust."

"It's a reminder of the importance of being heard," I say. "Stories need to be shared if they are to make a difference."

"I just worry no one's listening," Anil sighs. "Stories vanish without trace if they aren't read and passed on."

"Perhaps it's the reason why Queen Titania paves the way with dreams to keep the threads alive," I reply, thinking aloud. "Planting good ideas might miraculously turn them into wishes and action."

With a feeling of sudden positivity, Anil and I join the other sprites on the fairy trail home to puzzle over the Queen's task.

By the edge of the stream, Henry, a river sprite, paces thoughtfully, skimming stones across the rippling water. His brow furrows as he studies his reflection.

"The rule book is clear," he mutters, tugging a tattered guide from his satchel and flipping it open with a frown. "There's absolutely no room for interpretation. Just listen to this," he announces, clearing his throat, "*Sprites must* never *interfere with the material world. UNCW – UNDER NO CIRCUMSTANCES WHATSOEVER!*"

I hesitate. "But Queen Titania revised the rules at the Temple of the Winds. Anil and I were there when she made the decision. She might change them again."

Henry shoots me a sceptical look, as if I'd suggested something fantastical.

"Sky was one of the first to plant a dream as a seed of an idea," Anil adds proudly. "Given time, it will grow into something real."

Henry folds his arms in defiance. "Dreams are easily lost," he says. "And they're not the same as wishes. I wouldn't count on them."

"But dreams spark inspiration," I reply, standing my ground. "And inspiration *can* grow into something powerful in the material world. That's how change begins."

Henry sighs, his amber shine a little glow-lost, he glances at the stream, and I notice something shift in his expression.

"You're not wrong," he admits, his voice gentler. "But we'll need more than dreams to clean up the chemicals in our sewage-filled rivers. We'll have to step up and actually *do* something."

From the hedgerow, an ornithology sprite named Lark pipes up. "It's not only rivers, Henry, it's in the fields too. The soil can't breathe with chemical fertilisers. Nor can worms."

Another sprite, older, nods gravely. "Pesticides poison more than just pests, Lark. They poison the bees, and the birds, too, disrupting the natural balance of nature."

A bright white fledgling sprite files by, foraging. "Wishes for food that sustains life," she sings, trailing the scent of fennel and thyme behind her.

Henry's frown softens. "Hmm," he mumbles with thoughtful eyes. "Dreams filled with imaginative ideas… Farmers could find the strength to turn things around." He looks back at the stream, the sunlight dancing on the surface.

With a playful grin, he skips over a stone. "See you tomorrow," he calls, disappearing down the trail with a wave, the weight of the world momentarily lifted.

I glance at the peat-coloured stream in the twilight. An oily sheen clings to the surface, reflecting the last light and hinting at something chemical beneath. I dip my finger to check if the film will break caused by bacteria feeding on metals like copper. *Phew!* I sigh when it does not flow back into place. Just beyond, I spot a plastic shred snagged against a reed, carelessly discarded. I carefully remove it and take it home, hoping to find a use for it, knowing that it will never decompose or disappear.

As I get ready for bed, I haul up my balconies using the rope-pull mechanism, securing my home for the night. Once the final beam clicks into place, I feel the weight of responsibility pressing down on me. I worry that the path of achieving wishes without magic may be too steep for me to climb, and I can't shake my thoughts of letting our Queen down whispering in my mind.

Climbing into bed, I gaze up through the skylight. The hush of night has settled in. It's not quite silence, but more like a shift in the air, a pause, as if the wind is holding its breath, patiently waiting for something to happen. Jupiter shines steady and wise, while Mars flickers with restless energy. A shooting star, sudden, bold and gone in a moment, streaks across the sky. I quickly close my eyes and make a wish, not just for the magic I yearn for, but to help bring our world back into balance.

Far away, I know not where, the wind shifts direction. Without hearing a sound, I feel the Winds of Change beginning to stir.

* * *

Bathed in golden light, the first rays of dawn awaken me from sleep.

With a mug of mint tea in one hand, I lower my balcony with the other, as Anil arrives, ready for work. Even though it is the first day of our summer holidays, nature sprites never really take a break. Our duty is to remain vigilant and alert, ensuring harmony in nature wherever we turn.

Anil sets our journals on the table with pens, pencils and watercolours. Focusing our X-ray eyes, we pick up fine details at a glance. A willow-tit feasts on a dense colony of aphids, inadvertently protecting the tree from disease. I sketch its delicate wings, catching a glint of morning light. A kingfisher hovers, waiting to strike at darting minnows and dragonfly nymphs with its beak, its young calling for food from the safety of their burrow. Anil dips her brush into brilliant blue pigment, appreciating a chance to use it, making strokes that blur to mimic the rapid motion.

A fresh morning fragrance drifts through the trees, rich with the scent of damp soil and wildflowers. It lingers with the murmur of a far away call on the breeze. Anil tilts her head. "Did you hear that, Sky?" she asks, pricking up her ears.

I sniff the air; a gust of wind stirs the dry leaves, carrying whispers and vibrations of something new, which I can't quite place.

"What do you think it can be?" Anil asks, straining to hear.

I close my eyes to heighten my senses. "I know! At last," I say, "nature sprites of Northumberland are calling us to the celebration in Wonderland, uniting our fairy world with children."

Anil glows with excitement. "I knew it was something special! And," she says, pulling the Queen's card from her pocket and waving it in the air, "it must have something to do with this."

I disappear into the house to fetch my official invitation, reading it through. "Everyone will be there - from teachers, parents and children in the material world to teams of nature sprites that protect woodlands, wetlands, meadows, rivers, seas and valley mires on the moors. Traditional fairies, goblins, leprechauns, elves and pixies, not to mention Robbie the robin, are named on the invitation."

"Whoopee, wing and whirl - Wonderland, here we come!" Anil cheers, rushing off to collect her bags, her scarf streaming behind her like a superhero.

* * *

Ever since Anil and I headed for the Pixie Kingdom after our adventure with our team at the Temple of The Winds in Northern Ireland, we have patiently awaited the call to Wonderland. Siobhan and Clodagh, our hosts at Mount Stewart, had tucked our invitations away in our knapsacks and we only found them days later on our return home to Cabilla. It announced a gathering in the presence of Titania, Queen of the Fairies, in Wonderland, at the end of the rainbow in Northumberland. The dress code, described as 'self-expression', fuelled our imagination, and we immediately prepared to set off at a moment's notice.

I spot Robbie flying north as the rainbow takes shape.

"See you in Wonderland, Sky!" he whistles. "I'll be there well before you and Anil," he wagers, sweeping and swooping across the landscape.

Nature sprites emerge from tree homes flying in colour groups to add their unique glow to the rainbow. Anil's white light of youth had only recently transformed into a radiant violet when showing courage in the presence of Queen Titania at the Temple of the Winds. I collect my bag, and just as I am ready to leave, Anil returns with her backpack strapped under her wings.

"I haven't had much practice with rainbows," she says, a little shakily. "I hope I won't lose my balance!"

"All you need to remember is to hold on tight," I assure her.

At the speed of light, I wiggle my way into the yellows

alongside the oranges and reds, each sprite radiating the true colour of their nature. Gripping the hands of sprites beside her, Anil steadies herself at the edge of the violets as we embark on our journey.

"Goodbye, Bodmin," we call, heading over rolling hills towards Bristol. A whisper of excitement runs back and forth between us as gently as a breeze, our hair blown back, the wind sweeping us along our colourful paths on a comfortable cushion of air towards Wonderland, and the future Queen Titania is calling upon us to shape.

2

THE WONDER OF WISHES

Soaring through a kaleidoscope of colour, travelling at speed, we follow wavelengths of infrared light, riding along the shimmering arc towards the North Sea. Propelled by the Four Winds, the sun and the rain never leave our side, a symphony of the elements moving over an ever-changing landscape, traversing Birmingham, Sheffield, Leeds, Durham and Newcastle.

With a giggle and a bump, Anil and I slide off the end of the rainbow, tumbling straight into the enchantment of Wonderland.

"Flickeringfoxes!" we gasp.

Fairies with warm smiles greet us, handing out folded maps. The air smells of pine, rosemary and thyme, and tiny lanterns bob about like fireflies, illuminating the village alive with fashion and fun. Goblins, pixies and elves wander through the cobbled streets in britches, boots, feathered caps and berets. Some have long hair; others, cut short, loose, braided or shaved heads, with beards in every shape and size, cultivated like topiary hedges.

Swept along by the gentle flow of the crowd, we reach our sprite house – a mossy stone building twinkling with fairy lights. It overlooks a storytelling garden of wildflowers, and beyond it, we spot the Wishing Tree in full leaf.

Anil opens her plan of the village. "Liam's telling tales in the garden tomorrow," she says. "But where's he staying? I don't see a leprechaun cottage anywhere on the map."

Sprites perch at the doorway and lounge on the rounded rooftops, legs swinging, wings catching the last golden rays in the dusk.

"Hello, and welcome to Wonderland," smiles a garden sprite, checking names at a rose briar desk. "Bag a bed in a pod room and claim it with your pyjamas. Supper's in the Main Hall."

Anil and I marvel at the double-height space and the crisscross of wooden trusses that form geometric patterns between the upper rooms. Sprites perch on connecting beams, sipping soup, chattering below a roof insulated with moss and alive with lichen, fungi and algae. A glowing sign pulses with a passcode to join the mycelium network. Anil and I tune in.

Our cedar-scented pod room has bunk beds beside a circular window, moss mattresses and feather pillows placed as perfect lookout points to the Wishing Tree. We toss our pyjamas onto the pillows. *"Claimed!"* we shout, and scramble into our outfits. Anil buttons on her brown britches. I wiggle into my cherry-pink dress; eucalyptus leaves glimmering at the hem, releasing a fragrant aroma for children to sense our presence.

Entering the Main Hall, we catch kisses tossed towards us in welcome.

"You look lovely," calls a hospitality sprite, ladling nettle soup. "If you're quick, you'll catch the fashion parade before the gathering at the Wishing Tree."

"Let's find Pascal first," Anil suggests, squeezing my arm.

"No point," I grin. "Lydia sent a message to say he's socialising at the pixie palace all evening. Liam's bunking up on Pascal's boat – apparently he's become quite the seafarer these days."

We spot Kobalos near the entrance to the goblin grotto. Expressing his Grecian roots, he is elegantly dressed in a white cotton tunic, edged with the blue of the national flag, and matching pompom shoes.

"There you are!" he beams with open arms. "I stayed put, knowing you'd find me!"

"Smart move," I wink. "Keep that up, and you'll be telepathic by the end of summer."

Anil stands still. "Listen." She cups her ear. "The Wishing Tree is calling."

"Lydia, Layla and Anito are checking in at the sprite house and will meet us there," says Kobalos as we weave through the crowd. "We set sail from Northern Ireland this morning and docked the boat not far from here, next to guesthouses reserved for Woodland Welfare Workers."

"Miss Twig had better be here!" I shout.

"She is," he grins. "Asked me to join your lesson – '*How to inspire Wishes*' - first thing tomorrow."

"Crisis averted!" Anil calls out. "Children will be making wishes after breakfast, less than a sun-skip away, and we're totally unprepared!"

"Phew!" I gasp. "A lesson with Miss Twig is just the ticket! I haven't the foggiest how wishes actually work without using magic. Got any clues, Kobalos?"

"A few," he replies with a sideways glance. "Most folk think dreams come true just by wishing hard. But dreams are like gardens - they need tending. First, you plant the seed. Then, once they catch hold of the idea and believe in it, they will make it their own. But if they water the dream with doubt, it wilts." He pauses, looking me in the eye. "But if they nourish a dream with courage and determination, it blossoms into a wish that can grow stronger than they ever imagined."

"I see," I say softly, thinking it over.

"Wishes are empty dreams until someone acts upon them," he remarks as an afterthought. "But there's a danger. If a dream is blindly chased, it can become an obsession.

That's when people stop seeing clearly or noticing unexpected paths they could take. A wish provides a direction, but remaining open allows for flexibility to seize opportunities. That's how true magic happens."

We round a corner – and there it is. Bathed in moonlight, the Wishing Tree stands majestic, ancient limbs reaching skyward, leaves whispering secrets to the stars. Anil steps closer and runs her fingers reverently across the bark, reading the glowing patterns like a map.

"Positivity," she murmurs, "… mixed with unease. Encouragement, without answers."

Illuminated by fairy lights, signs hang from the branches, while others cling to the honeydew left by insects on the bark. Among them are wishes for courage, healing, and happiness. A larger sign, sways gently in the breeze: *Wishes to Mend the Material World: Needing Less, Sharing More and Listening to Nature.*

Lydia floats down in a colourful kanga wrap, her shuka shawl swirling around her blue aura like music. Layla follows, her yellow and blue tunic brushing against the air, her radiant shine shimmering indigo, tinged with red. Next, Anito appears, glowing green in a collarless Kurta and loose trousers. We hug beneath the sign, our thoughts flowing between us like ripples in water. It is not in spite of our cultural differences that we belong together; it is because of them. Unique ideas from each of us bounce between us like rays of light, with every voice needed, each one integral to the whole. The wish that sways above our heads isn't just an idea; it's the reason we are here.

"Wishes are magically filtered by traditional fairies," Lydia explains gently. "They guide the wishes to the nature sprite they are meant for, to catch."

"I hope Miss Twig explains what we're meant to do after that," I murmur. "I still don't have a clue of how to make a single wish come true."

"Trust your instincts," suggests Kobalos. "When belief is rooted in truth, wishes gain their wings. A single whisper of doubt must be kept out at all costs!"

Suddenly, I burst out laughing. "Look!" I shout, pointing as Liam somersaults out from under a bush in a flurry of movement and strikes a comical pose.

"Hello!" he calls, brushing himself down, grabbing his hat as a gust nearly carries it off. "That's my cue," he calls, retrieving a brass bell from a table beside a floral thrown.

He rings it with all the ceremony of a royal announcement. "Oyez, oyez! Nature sprites and traditional fairies, please take your places on your branches. Titania, Queen of the Fairies, will soon grace us with her presence."

We quickly scramble to take our positions. Fluttering with anticipation, all eyes turn to the edge of the clearing. A sea mist emerges, initially glowing softly, becoming dazzlingly bright. Queen Titania rides the breeze, radiant in a gown of white petals. Her crystal crown sparkles in the moonlight, and her curls cascade over her shoulders as she takes her place on the throne of wildflowers. Radiating confidence and calm, she makes us shine a little brighter.

"Today we mark a new era of hope," she says, her voice clear and warm. "Traditional fairies will take responsibility for wishes they grant. Nature sprites will learn to plant dreams that inspire wishes to help nature in the material world."

A quiet ripple stirs the branches.

"A wish," she continues, "is never an order. It's a spark, a possibility."

A hush falls over the grove. The Queen pauses, allowing the silence to draw us closer.

"Inspiring wishes with dreams is an art," she says. "Sprites will learn how to help wishes for clean rivers, fresh air, and a world free of plastic waste come true. These are wishes made every day – and yet, right now, so few come through."

We exchange uneasy glances.

"They fade," Titania says softly, "because people forget they have power. They toss their wishes into the Universe like pennies into a well… and then they wait." She leans forward, her eyes shining. "That's why you are here. To remind the material world that magic isn't in waiting – it's in doing. Birds carry warnings. Trees pass messages of danger. And the Four Winds – North, South, East and West – rise in protest. Their breezes become cries, and their whispers swell into storms of confusion."

A hush settles as she steps forward, her gown catching the light.

"The time of thoughtless wishing has passed," she says, her voice calm but commanding. "No more wishes for mountains of toys or fast fashion that ends up forgotten and thrown away. Those kinds of wishes don't bring joy – they bring clutter and harm. It's time to listen out for wishes that count."

She holds up her head as a gust of wind stirs a flurry of leaves.

"There are dreams that sprites must learn to plant, ready to grow into wishes," she commands. "Dreams of climbing trees, building dens from fallen branches, making mud pies, and swimming in rivers so clean you can see the pebbles at the bottom. These are dreams that childhoods should be made of. Not dreams of plastic throw away items that break by bedtime." Queen Titania steps back, her voice softening. "Let's show them a world where playing in the park, making homemade crowns, and sharing laughter feels like magic – because it is." She lifts her chin, her voice rising like a song. "Yes, there is the brightest kind of hope that lives in children - in their laughter, dreams and curiosity, in their endless questions. These are not small things. They are strands of real magic, strong enough to help heal the world. But they can't do it alone. Children need us, and we need them."

A hush falls over the tree.

"Sprites and fairies are the bridge between our

worlds," she says. "You can inspire belief, not just in wishing, but in the courage to act. Help children's magic blossom alongside their confidence, so they feel strong enough to change the world."

Her gaze sharpens, her voice becoming clearer and stronger.

"And protect them," she adds, "from Murmurers who whisper doubt into their ears. The path ahead won't be easy. The forces confusing the Winds are clever. They stir doubt, delay, and distract. The material world is filled with choices, but not all of them are wise. You must help children find clarity. Show them that one small, kind action can ripple outwards. Offer them a picture of a better way – brighter, wider and more real than anything they've ever wished for."

"Can't she just give us some magic?" Anil whispers.

I grin, but it's Titania who answers, her smile full of knowledge.

"The magic is already there – in children," she says. "If each of you inspires just one true dream that takes root, the fog will lift. Many hands make light work. The Winds may have lost their way, but with nature sprites guiding behaviour like a compass, the world can still return to harmony."

The Queen stands tall, her wings shimmering in the moonlight.

"Traditional fairies may still wave their wands to grant wishes," she says warmly, 'but we're starting something new and important." Titania turns towards a clearing and gestures to a wooden sign beside the ancient tree.

"I am introducing a new golden rule," she declares, her voice bright. She points to the bold words painted on the sign.

Wishes for material things will no longer be granted!

A stunned buzz of disbelief ripples through the branches – a wind sweeping across a restless sea. Shocked gasps disrupt the air. Even the most graceful fairies cover their mouths in horror. One senior fairy lets out a dramatic sigh and drops down onto a toadstool, fanning his face and shaking his head.

"But don't worry," Titania says, turning towards him. "You will grant only the very best of wishes, the kind that help others, protect nature, and make people feel loved by bringing joy. These are the wishes that truly matter."

"But it's our tradition," he protests, his voice cracking. "It's what we're known for."

The Queen lifts her hand. Instantly, we fall silent.

"The time has come for change," she says, her tone gentle but firm. "Material things have given humans moments of delight, yes... but too often, they have left behind emptiness, comparison and division. The endless hunger for more has dulled hearts that once knew how to feel full. Benchmarks of frivolity have replaced the true measures of happiness."

She lets the silence speak, heavy and full of reflection.

"Sprites will help guide wishes," the Queen continues softly, "towards ones that truly count - the quiet ones. The ones that call for more than magic – that call for meaning."

"Meaning?" pipes up a baffled fairy. "But how will sprites do that?"

The Queen turns towards the tree, now faintly glowing beneath the starlight. Her voice grows steady.

"By planting the seeds of dreams that grow the deepest wishes," she says. "Wishes for peace – so people may find a path to walk together. Wishes for justice – that begins with listening and grows into courage. Wishes for respect – to honour our differences and bind us in understanding. And wishes for love… most of all, for the love of the natural world."

She lifts her gaze higher, as if addressing the stars.

"Without nature, there is no life. No future. Humans are not separate from the Earth; they are woven into its fabric, part of the great family of living things. To forget that is to forget themselves. It is not the material world that will save them. It is the natural world that must win through. And it is our task to keep that hope alive."

She looks at each of us, her voice anchored in the moment. "These wishes may not come true right away, but will act as signposts. The more people who follow them – children, families and communities – the more they become real. That is the magic. Not in what is granted, but in what is *grown*. From now on," she proclaims, "wishes that ask for more 'stuff' will fade in the wind. But wishes that ask for purpose, to help others, to restore nature, to reuse, rebuild and repair, will shimmer with potential and power."

Fairies fidget on their branches, some clearly preferring the old ways. Sensing their unrest, the Queen settles regally on the throne. "Imagine giving the gift of courage to face a fear or the strength to keep going when the road is hard. The creativity to untangle problems, and the wisdom to see beauty where others see nothing at all." She pauses, her gaze fixed. "And kindness – not just as a polite gesture, but as a warm light reaching someone who feels forgotten, a quiet reminder that they matter and are not alone. Sometimes, a single act of kindness is enough to lift the heavy curtain of loneliness and let the sunlight back in. Or a spark of hope, just enough to ignite a dream."

A hush sweeps through the fairies like a gentle breeze. "These," she concludes, her voice rich with certainty, "are the wishes we must bring to life, for they are the roots of true magic. And they grow deeper than anything glittering gold could ever provide."

A fairy draped in jasmine blossom drifts down, her sweet scent calming the air. She curtsies deeply before the Queen.

"Your Majesty," she says, "material gifts are still all children wish for. As guardians of our fairy godchildren, what shall we do to avoid disappointment?"

The Queen's smile sends a glow or warmth. "They

may resist at first. But we must show them the power of gifts that cannot be held in their hands, only in their hearts. These are the gifts that truly endure. Imagine a child wishing to overcome shyness, to find the confidence to read aloud in class, or the strength to bounce back from failure. *These* are treasures that last a lifetime and wishes traditional fairies may readily grant."

The air stills. Wings flutter as heads turn, the Queen's words settling in our thoughts.

"A wish for courage," says a fairy, his voice clear, "could change a life."

"And a wish for hope," adds another with eyes glistening, "might save one."

The Queen nods, solemn and proud. "Yes, these wishes are vital and must be caught. Sprites will help guide dreams that can transform into wishes and come true."

"I don't get it," Anil mutters under her breath. "How can we change what children wish for?"

The Queen's voice turns grave. "Since the nature sprites united nations with rainbows and pledged to reduce pollution… emissions have still risen. Traditional fairies, without meaning to, have encouraged this by granting wishes for material possessions, especially for plastic toys, which harm the Earth."

A wave of concern sweeps through the gathering like a sudden gust.

"Excuse me, Your Majesty," I ask, trying to sound braver than I feel. "How will children adapt without toys?"

The Queen's expression softens. "We're not taking their toys away. We're inviting them to treasure what they already have and to share their favourites in schools, clubs and toy libraries. We'll help guide them back to outdoor play, to imagination, connecting back to nature. It's good for their health, and for the planet, too."

She leans forward, her voice a conspiratorial whisper.

"You see, when someone buys a toy, a gadget, a shiny thing, they only pay the price on the label, which does not take into account the damage the product has caused to nature to make it, nor the waste it leaves behind. These costs are paid by our rivers, forests, and oceans."

We shake our heads.

"So imagine," she says, her voice warming up, "if the real cost was counted – not just in coins, but in clean air, coral reefs, and polar ice. Then plastic would become more expensive than gold. And people would start to choose differently, and wisely. Choosing things made with care, that belong to a natural ecosystem."

A clear-sky fairy in a lavender-smocked dress steps forward with a furrowed brow. "But what will children play with?"

The Queen smiles, her eyes twinkle. "With one another. Using their imagination, playing ball, making camps, telling stories under trees. Completing puzzles, passing down cherished toys. Playing make-believe, sharing wild adventures in playgrounds. And when they do need something new, they'll choose it carefully, knowing the planet pays a price."

I raise my hand. "And where do we find the magic?"

"It's already here," the Queen replies. "Good wishes come true with conviction. It's a deeper kind of magic, and we'll need it. Mother Earth is reaching her tipping point of no return," she sighs. "For over two hundred years, factories have churned out cheap goods at a high cost to nature. The Earth did not demand payment, and for a long time, the damage went unchecked. But now, the Four Winds are stirring, demanding an end to this behaviour in the only way they know how: with floods, storms, landslides and wildfires."

Anil steps forward, her voice urgent.

"The oceans are warming. Acidification is killing the coral reefs – bleached and brittle. Greenland and Antarctica are melting. Sea levels are rising. The planet needs cooling, and fast."

Lydia lifts her chin.

"Your Majesty, at the Temple of the Winds in Northern Ireland, my proposal for a global nature pact was agreed. But zilch happened."

"Do not despair," the Queen replies calmly. "The human quest to restore its bond with nature is gathering steam. A World Climate Forum is planned by caring people to give nature a stronger voice and help measure the true costs. And, another is underway to enforce a Global Plastics Treaty. Challenges," she adds with serenity, "are simply opportunities in disguise. The Winds of Change are already stirring."

"'*Winds of Change*'," Anil repeats, eyes brightening. "The Four Winds could really use their help."

"At dawn," says the Queen, her voice soft with promise, "you'll gather at the Wishing Tree with your teachers. Draw strength from it. Soon, you'll be helping children everywhere wish differently, wishing wisely, not like the wasted wishes often described in fairy tales."

A hush falls again. I feel the weight of our task sink in. Quietly, I whisper a wish, asking the tree for courage. Then, gently, the Queen adds: "And when it comes to food… it's no different. Cheap food comes at an environmental cost, which ought to be added to the unit price of food that is grown, but like plastic, it isn't. Why? Because profit is the name of the game, overruling everything else."

The Queen sighs. "Children should know what it feels like to be truly nourished. But many companies add sugar to make food taste better – not to help children grow, but to sell more. Too much sugar can leave children feeling tired, moody, or even unwell.

"Instead, let's help them discover the natural sweetness of juicy pears, sun-ripened strawberries, crisp apples, as well as nuts and raisins. Encourage them to enjoy the vibrant colours of vegetables, the comfort of homemade meals, and to drink clear, fresh tap water instead of sugary drinks.

"Crisps and packaged treats might seem fun, but they often cost more than they're worth. And when eaten daily, they can do more harm than good."

The Queen pauses, then softly adds: "Don't blame children for their choices. Inspire them. Show them how real food gives them strength and focus. Together, we can change the way food is grown and shared to help every child thrive."

"What about the celebration? Will there be any cake?" Anil asks hopefully, sharing an image of a party horn and tables piled high with cupcakes and jellies.

The Queen gives a slight tilt of her head.

"Of course. There'll be tea and home baked cake in the storytelling garden, served with scones and jam tarts as a treat," she smiles. "Tomorrow, Miss Twig will teach you how to make wishes truly take shape. And at three o'clock, Liam the leprechaun will share true tales of renewal."

Titania looks up in solemn serenity.

"It's time for change to begin. And you'll soon see how, miraculously, the pieces of the puzzle come together."

As the last word leaves her lips, a sudden shiver runs through the air. The breeze dies down into an eerie stillness. We hear a crackle, not thunder or lightening, but something deeper, like static electricity tangled with whispering voices. From beyond the clearing, a shadow flickers like a flame.

Anil inches closer, her hand brushing against mine.

"Did you hear that?" she whispers, her voice tight.

We turn. The tree's golden sign begins to dim, as if a veil has passed across the moon. A cold gust twists through the branches. From the shadows, a voice, brittle and sharp slithers into the hush.

"Wishes?" it mocks. "Let's see what the children *really* wish for…"

Louder murmuring starts to build, coming not from the sprites, but from somewhere else. The Queen stiffens, rising once more.

"They've returned," she says grimly. "The Murmurers."

A hush falls over us once more, but this time, it is anything but gentle.

3

DREAMS THAT COME TRUE

Sharing a room with my sister means whispering and chattering into the night without much sleep.

"I'm scared that I'll mess up, Sky," Anil says, pulling the blanket up to her chin. "I don't really understand the wish thing. I need a few clues." Her voice trembles. "I'm scared of the Murmurers. The Queen was right. They're back, whispering doubts, stirring confusion."

I slip out of bed and perch on the windowsill, hugging my knees. The wind has settled into a gentle whisper, soft and steady.

"They always show up when change is close," I say quietly. "We mustn't let them stop us, Anil. A soil sprite I met today named Sol said that confusion never takes root in thriving places, where people believe in each other. He teams up with sprites to inspire more than one idea in a single dream, aiming to spread them far and wide and make a real difference. He says that if enough of us act, the Murmurers will be swept away by the momentum of thriving ecosystems living in harmony with nature around the world."

Anil peeks out from beneath the covers, her face pale in the moonlight.

"It's not that easy, Sky. It's fine for us - we live in a temperate climate and should count ourselves lucky, but many sprites overseas suffer from extreme weather," she whispers.

"What's more, they asked for help, and we've let them down," I reply, lowering my eyes in shame. "Catching that wish at the nature summit made it my responsibility. And now…" I open the window. Cool air rushes in. Outside, the Wishing Tree sways gently under the silver moon.

"Nations made promises," Anil interrupts, sitting up in bed. "To cut pollution. But tonight, the Queen said they'd only increased it. I'm not sure what you were supposed to do with the wish once you caught it, anyway, Sky."

"That's half the problem," I whisper, climbing back under the covers. "But doing something, rather than nothing, would have been a start."

"Sprites united in making a promise to change the world with rainbows stretching across continents," Anil says looking up. "You can't expect to do it alone, Sky."

"The sprites that spoke at the nature summit were desperate. They said we only have ten, maybe twenty years to prevent irreversible damage - ice melting, habitats disappearing for walruses and polar bears. And in the Middle East, the heat is so fierce they can hardly breathe at times. I should have done something by now, Anil," I sigh, wingheavy and downcast.

She yawns, snuggling into her pillow. "It's never too late, Sky. The summit wasn't the end; it was only the beginning. The seeds are already there in thoughts and minds. To actively cool the planet, it's up to us to help them grow."

I close my eyes, but my mind won't settle. Images flicker and blur: forests gasping for breath, rivers choking on waste, glaciers weeping into the sea. Somewhere between waking and sleep, a dream takes shape. A mist rolls above a swelling ocean. A duck named Salter bobs bravely on the waves, navigating swirling currents, surfing through dwindling ice across a vast expanse of rising sea…

Salter's face shifted from stern to gentle or lost in thought. His sharp eyes cut through the haze, and his brisk, clipped words, commanding urgent requests, rebound across the waves.

"You need to act, Sky. No more delays," he urges, flapping his wings in distress. "I'm dead to the world and need your help more than ever."

"Help you? What can I possibly do?" I ask, startled and flustered.

"I've heard you can make wishes come true, by

planting dreams," he says.

"Well, maybe, but I don't exactly know how," I admit uneasily. "Anyway, what are you doing in my dream?"

"It's the only way I can reach the material world," he replies matter-of-factly. "You're attuned to the wishes I need you to catch at the Wishing Tree. So catch them!"

"I see," I say, remembering him from a dream of sailing across a sea of melting ice. "You demonstrated your work with the Winds and showed how they throw sea water high into the air to rebrighten clouds that reflect sunlight away from Earth, bringing down sea temperatures, and cooling the planet."

"Quite so," Salter replies with a satisfied nod of approval. "Now, we must take the next step with a fleet of unmanned ships that spray fine seawater droplets into the atmosphere. They'll create the necessary clouds to reflect sunlight away from Earth and help cool the planet."

"I remember the demonstration. It was a vivid dream," I confirm. "You impressed me by saying you weren't afraid to speak your truth and save the Four Winds," I remind him. "But isn't interfering with the weather rather risky?"

"Burning coal is risky!" he snaps. "We need to work with nature, not against it. I can harness wave energy to create clouds, providing shade during summer daylight at the North Pole."

"Building ships takes time. Couldn't existing ones be

converted, instead?" I suggest.

Salter turns sharply towards me, surprised. "Well, that's quite an idea, Sky," he says, raising an eyebrow. "And I'll tell you why. A few years back, an international law was passed to reduce sulphur emissions from ships by 80%, with clear benefits to air quality and human health."

"Sounds good," I say.

"Well, yes and no," he replies, locking eyes with me. "It also meant that there are fewer sulphate particles in the clean air to help form clouds, and a smaller number of droplets in these clouds, reduces the amount of solar radiation reflected back into space."

"Ah ha," I say, catching on. "So you aim to replace the sulphur with natural seawater containing tiny particles of salt?"

"Quite so," he quacks with satisfaction. "However, it is no longer an *aim* but a necessity."

"I like the idea of nature-based solutions as long as it doesn't interfere with the weather, but isn't that the job of the Four Winds, not spray boats?" I ask.

"Industrial manufacture is what I call interfering with the weather," Salter retorts, smoothing his feathers. "I am a scientist. And for your information, my invention," he adds with a wry smile, "is bio-mimicry. It means working with nature. It may be a wild card, but it could also be played as a trump. Play it!"

"Problems with the weather are escalating," I say. "But is your idea really a solution?"

"It's *the* solution," he insists with annoyance, "...to buy us the time to recover and transition to clean energy. Spread the word, Sky. Gather support to bring my invention to life."

"But how?" I ask, overwhelmed. "I don't even know where to start and it is not up to me. Some will strongly oppose it and the fairy world is not allowed to get involved in any crossfire."

"Catch the wishes that align with this mission, and get yourself to the Pixie Kingdom. Make it happen!" he says briskly. "The dinner on Monday evening in the grand house in the square is hosted by The Lady and the house owner. Important guests will be present," he informs me.

"The Pixie Kingdom?" I gasp. "You mean the dream I planted is coming to life?"

"Yes! The Earth is heating up faster than anyone expected, and action is urgent. Support from the insurance sector is the key. I'll be in touch through your dreams," he says, his determined voice barely audible over the roar of the ocean, as he fearlessly rides an enormous wave into the distance. Insurance? I don't even know what that means.

* * *

As the morning light filters through the leaves, our sprite house begins to stir, pulling me gently from sleep as the remnants of my vivid dream dissolve into the sounds of a new day. Birdsong wafts in, led by Robbie the robin, perched like a sentry on a branch outside our window. His clear, unwavering call signals it is time for our tutorial. I glance past the Wishing Tree to the woodland beyond, bathed in warm golden light, and in the quiet stillness, a familiar voice drifts through my mind, resolute and clear: *no more delays.*

Anil sits up on the bunk bed below me.

"Weird dreams again?" she mumbles, rubbing the sleep from her eyes.

"Yes," I nod. "But not so much weird this time… more like urgent."

Anil climbs the ladder and peers over the top, her voice still drowsy. "I dreamt of whispers last night… but not voices I recognised."

"You mean the Murmurers," I say quietly. "Like the Queen warned us. It's because you went to sleep thinking about them and allowed them in."

Anil shivers.

"They feed on doubt," I add, brushing hair away from my face.

She nods slowly. "Then we'd better keep our thoughts clear. There's no room for fog." She climbs back down. "What kind of urgent dream did you have?" she asks, but I never get the chance to answer. The sunlight wanes, dimming as a shadow flits past the window. A scent clings to the air – faint but unmistakable: smoke. There's a flutter, a murmur - not birdsong, but something else entirely – a chill wind that feels out of place. I inhale sharply, but my breath catches. *I know I won't be able to make wishes come true. Not without magic.* I frown, trying to push the thought away.

"They're stirring," I whisper. "The Murmurers. I think they know we're getting ready to act. Don't allow them in, Anil. We've got to block them out somehow, or we'll never get anything done."

* * *

Maximus awoke with a jolt on the morning of the rainbow that led to Wonderland, his heart racing from a vivid dream that felt like a glimpse into the future. In it, he lived in perfect harmony with nature – a life he had never considered before, yet now it tugged at something quietly nestled in the back of his mind.

At first, he dismissed it as fanciful nonsense, but the dream continued to linger in his thoughts, becoming more and more significant. Unbeknown to Max, as he preferred to be known, his vast estate was home to a close-knit community of sprites dedicated to nurturing the soil, woodlands, meadows, gardens, and his farm. The sprites were intent on reversing the impact of industrialised agriculture on the climate, their common goal to restore biodiverse communities of insects and microorganisms in healthy soil and plants. He was also unaware that Titania, Queen of the Fairies, had granted sprites the power to plant seeds of dreams into human minds, inspiring them to reconnect with nature and care for the natural world.

When Max fell asleep, sprites gathered at his bedside, weaving a vision into his subconscious. Each sprite contributed an idea, creating a tapestry of orchards heavy with fruit, meadows buzzing with bees, clear rivers, and wildflowers swaying in the breeze - not just in his own surroundings, but everywhere. Satisfied with their work, the sprites slipped away, leaving Max to nurture the dream and develop it in his own unique way.

Wide-awake, fragments of the dream clung to him, urging him to see his estate differently. Tying his dressing gown, Max steps onto the balcony. Braced by the sharp morning air, he watches birds glide across the meticulously manicured lawn. A bee hovers over a rebellious clump of clover that had escaped the last dose of weed killer, and a butterfly flitters onto a daisy. Instead of anger, a wistful smile creeps across his lips. For the first time, he doesn't see weeds; he sees the life they attract.

"Ah, yes," Max murmurs. "No more mowing; we'll let the wildflowers and long grasses blow free in the wind. Brambles and dog rose will flourish in the hedgerows, creating homes for birds and hedgehogs. I'll plant an orchard with apples, pears and plums – trees that bloom in their own time to withstand rogue frosts instead of wiping them all out at once. And I'll keep just enough lawn for croquet and lawn tennis." His voice grows firmer, lighter. "No more chemicals," he says, sweeping his gaze across the 1,000-acre estate bathed in sunshine. "No more weedkiller polluting the groundwater and harming pollinators, earthworms and the soil itself. I want to regenerate with rich soil and grow nutritious food."

He taps his head with the sudden realisation that he had been trying to control something greater than himself, when he should have been working with nature as a helpful partner instead. His newfound vision fills his mind with ideas springing up like young shoots.

"Along the riverbanks, I'll plant water-hyacinth, water lettuce, water mint, with ferns and grasses, not simply for erosion control, but to filter the water of toxins caused by chemicals choking the river of life. What's more, I'll turn my chlorinated swimming pool into a lily pond with carp, reeds, rushes and ramps, where frogs and hedgehogs can feed on slugs, instead of them finding their way to my vegetable garden."

He stands still - tall, lean, and radiant. It's as if a light has flicked on inside him. Each idea unfolds a new pathway, branching towards a future he wants to shape. Awash with new emotions, a lone tear trickles down his cheek. He wipes it away with the back of his hand and lifts his gaze, searching for something intangible that he cannot identify.

The sprites that planted the dream into his mind had hopes of their own. Led by a soil sprite named Sol, they believed their vision for Max's dream would spark a revelation within him. But, they did not anticipate the quiet ache that lingered beneath his carefully crafted façade. Although Max seemed to have everything anyone could ever wish for, the sprites saw that with all his land and privilege, no material possessions or trappings of wealth could fill the emptiness inside him. When the sprites saw a single tear trace its way down Max's cheek, they knew the dream had taken root, no longer just an idea, but a quiet awakening. Something within him had shifted, gently and irreversibly. Awakened to the beauty of nature, Max felt a sudden, soaring sense of freedom he'd never known before. Not the freedom of escape, but one found in belonging, of mattering, of being part of something vast, beautiful and alive. In that moment, Max understood he was not separate from nature but woven into its fabric.

The sharp scent of rain, warmed by rays of sunshine, catch Max's attention. A vibrant rainbow arches across the sky, shimmering with intense colours that stop Max in his tracks. The hues seem alive, pulsing with energy in an arc so expansive that Max wonders whether it is an optical illusion.

Suddenly, a memory struck him like lightning. "The invitation!" he exclaims, spinning on his heel and rushing back inside. He tears through his desk drawers, scattering papers onto the floor, but finds nothing. Recalling the envelope sealed with wax, the ornate coat of arms and his name scrawled in ink, he casts his mind back to retrace his steps.

"Of course!" He bolts down the corridor, through the main hall, past the staircase, and into the drawing room. The rhythmic ticking of the clock on the mantelpiece fills the air.

Max rifts through a stack of invitations, his heart pounding. Finally, he finds it.

"By Jingo, here it is!" he cries, holding the card aloft. The handwritten instructions on the back are clear: he has to act now. Snatching a painted porcelain box from the table, Max flings open the French windows and dashes onto the rain-soaked lawn. The downpour doesn't deter him; the rainbow shimmers like a beacon, calling him to action.

Whatever lies ahead, Max knows this is his moment. The dream had planted the seed, but now it was up to him to make it grow. Determined to guide him further, the sprites head towards the glowing rainbow, eager to reach Wonderland before Max, ready to help him uncover the true happiness he seeks.

THE SOCIETY OF ORIGINAL THINKERS

Invites you to a celebration in Wonderland at the end of the rainbow, Northumberland,
in the presence of Titania, Queen of the Fairies,

UNITING THE FANTASY WORLDS OF FAIRIES AND CHILDREN
to help make wishes come true.
Maximus

....

Special thanks for contributions from
Supporting teams, including sprites, fairies, goblins, leprechauns, elves, pixies and a robin, named Robbie.

Defenders of the Four Winds will be very welcome.
'Les résolveurs de notre temps' are cordially invited to apply for membership of the
Direct Climate Cooling Initiative, attending dinner in rue Ducale upon application.

RSVP:
Fairy godchildren, their teachers and
Industry leaders are invited to apply for tickets.

Dress code: Self-Expression

"Phew!" Max sighs with relief, catching his breath as the rainbow continues to glow brightly across the sky. Tiny flakes of fairy dust, illuminated by shafts of golden sunlight, dance through the raindrops, shimmering like fragments of a dream.

Holding his index finger to gauge the wind's direction, Max pulls a cotton handkerchief from his pocket. With careful precision, he stretches it loosely between his fingers and thumbs, creating a makeshift sail. The breeze catches, carrying seeds of hope – tiny, glistening specks seeking fertile minds to plant themselves. Max carefully shakes the precious cargo into his porcelain box, its delicate lid snapping shut with a satisfying click.

With curiosity and purpose in his eyes, still in his dressing gown and pyjamas, Max tucks the porcelain box into his pocket, striding out through the misty rain, his heart beating with anticipation.

What lay at the end of the rainbow? What did it mean to bridge the realms of human imagination and the magical world of fairies? And why, of all people, had he been chosen for such an extraordinary journey?

He didn't yet have the answers, but as Max set off into the sunlit drizzle, he felt certain of one thing: his life was about to change forever.

4

THE WISHING TREE

The Wishing Tree sparkles with the bright white light of fairies and the colourful glow of nature sprites, a sight so enchanting it takes Miss Twig's breath away. Clasping her hands in awe, she makes a wish that urges us to listen closely.

"Before we explore the magic of wishes," she begins, "remember that dreams must be planted to unlock the wish-maker's imagination if they are to become true."

Sol leans over. "I'd like to inspire a wish for communal compost for worms to enjoy, helping communities grow nutritious vegetables to share," he whispers.

Miss Twig turns her gaze towards us. "Every part of an ecosystem is equally important. Worms perform their role; beetles fulfil theirs; and microorganisms, though invisible, are vital contributors to a compost heap, a kingdom all of its own. Plant dreams that resonate, inspiring the dreamer to accomplish them as wishes that can come true."

Sol sends me an image of thriving vegetables grown in a woodland clearing, animals grazing beneath the trees.

"Collaborate, by all means," says Miss Twig. "But, before planting a dream, use your intuition to shape them for the maximum benefit of nature."

"What if it's too hard for the dreamer to take on?" Sol asks.

"Nothing is impossible if you help them believe in themselves," Miss Twig assures us. "Plant dreams like seeds, tied to something they can grasp and hold onto, so they don't give up before they've even begun. It's the effort that matters most; determination turns the impossible into the possible, step by step. Think of it like knitting a complex pattern, one stitch after another, row by row, from what once seemed like a ball of tangled threads. When a wish is no longer a longing but begins to take shape as a purpose, it's on the verge of becoming real," she determines. "Action is crucial. Once a good idea is born, it seeks the light like a seedling driven to grow and take root. More magic comes when it transforms into what sprites call a *Glowgrow* when an idea refuses to stay small and starts changing the world, one thought at a time. Given a chance, it gains the courage to find its way into minds, hearts, and actions."

We flap our wings in quiet applause.

"Once you work on a few," she adds brightly, "you'll soon realise that the wish-maker finds value in making choices, strengthening their will to succeed. Their only real enemy is doubt, and it takes strength of character to overcome it."

I raise my hand. "Miss Twig, please give us an example?"

"In truth, Sky, you must figure out each wish for yourself. Unique to the wish-maker, start with ideas they genuinely care about to allow the dreamer to develop them into their own real wishes. Your keen intuition and ability to read their thoughts will help you plant dreams that are sure to take root. Here at the Wishing Tree, the wish comes first. All you need to do is catch it and assist them in pursuing it. Remember, the wish-maker must fulfil their wish; that's not *your* responsibility. Only they can shape their thoughts and align their dreams with reality through determination, including those you've planted to inspire them."

Miss Twig pauses. "Remember, worrying about the future is like trying to predict where a seed will land and whether it will grow. Don't waste time guessing where the wind will blow; get down to hard work, and the rest will follow."

* * *

Sitting on our branch with a sense of unease, Anil and I watch as children, parents and teachers gather around the base of the Wishing Tree. Fairy godparents settle on nearby branches, unsure of what to expect. We learn that fairies will filter wishes like magnets, drawn to those of us best able to make them a reality.

Wishes begin to float up – sparkling, transparent orbs that shimmer. Anil catches the first one drawn to her.

"It's from Claudia," Anil bursts out with urgency. "She wishes to save hedgehogs, which face threats from traffic and loss of habitat."

"I love hedgehogs," I reply, tilting my head in thought. "But what can you do to help her wish come true?"

"Not much," Anil answers. "Claudia will handle it herself. She's already envisioning a homemade safety crossing and has plans to engage her neighbourhood. Her idea is to create feeding stations by making simple changes to gardens that will benefit hedgehogs. She's even thought of putting small holes in fences and ramps in ponds, as well as encouraging people to stop using slug pellets, which often kill them. It's awesome! I don't have to do anything at all!"

"Wow! Claudia nailed it!" I blink in amazement. "We need more people like her who have vision."

"Exactly," Anil nods. "Claudia intends to agree official road signs to protect hedgehogs everywhere. Go on, Sky," she encourages me with a smile. "Catch the next wish that comes your way."

I spot a wish caught on the branch and am automatically attracted to it. I do as Anil suggests and open it, stunned that it is a wish I would have made myself, but have no idea of how to fulfil it. And then I remember my dream about the duck named Salter. I tuck it away for later.

Suddenly, another wish comes hurtling towards me: *I wish to regenerate my land to grow nutritious food*, it says.

Panic sets in. I don't know how to help with that wish either. Deciding to seek advice from Kobalos, I'm relieved to find him at a picnic bench, enjoying the sun.

"How are you doing?" he asks with a smile.

"Not well," I confess. "I'm stuck on my wishes and afraid I'll let everyone down."

"Don't be ridiculous. Remember, you can't fulfil a wish for someone else. They need to work it through for themselves. Your job is to help them cultivate their ideas. I can't give you the answers – you have to find your own way, Sky," Kobalos explains.

"But I have two impossible, unrelated wishes to resolve!" A knot tightens in my chest, accompanied by a fear I can't quite identify. "I'm stuck, Kobalos, and a nagging voice keeps telling me I'm not cut out for this," I whisper, my voice barely audible. "I just don't know what to do."

He studies me for a moment. "The trick is to keep learning, yes - but never lose your ability to build things that matter – ideas, friendships, solutions no one's tried before, even before you think you're ready." He crouches down and draws a spiral in the earth with a stick. "Do you know the thing about true leaders, Sky?" he asks, not looking up. "They don't wait until they've been trained or told. Oh no. They step forward *because* no one else has been brave enough to show the way." He glances up. "Leaders are the ones who notice something's missing – a broken system no one is fixing, a solution waiting to be seen, or a clever idea no one's tried. And instead of waiting for permission, they begin, led by their heart." He passes me the stick. "People think leaders have to be experts – trained, tested, all figured out. But most of the best ones?" Kobalos gives a gravelly chuckle. "They start out just like you. With a question no one's answering, a dream too strange for others to understand, and the bravery to try, even if they tumble into obstacles they'll have to overcome." He taps me gently on the forehead. "So don't wait to be ready. Just be *willing*. That's how the world begins to change."

He looks me square in the eye.

"And beware the Murmurers, sneaking in when you're tired. They thrive on bright minds and twist courage into fog. But here's the thing – every time they appear, you'll learn a little more about how to deal with them. That's how it works, Sky. You don't start out knowing everything. You find out what you're made of along the way, step by step, choice by choice. You've got this, Sky."

"I don't think I have, Kobalos."

"I disagree. Sometimes, when the Murmurers catch a whiff of a good heart, they creep close and whisper failure into your mind," Kobalos says. "You must learn to spot their tricks – they're full of fog and fear, nothing more. They are easily dissipated with a will to be rid of them. Keep your focus. After all, there's no timescale for finding the answers. Put the wishes in your pocket and take your time over them.

Why not fly off to a quiet place where a solution will surely come to you?"

Feeling better and following Kobalos's advice, I head for The Cheviot, an extinct volcano in the hills near the Scottish border. Eight hundred metres above sea level, I can see the hills of Northumberland rolling into the distance. But right there in the foreground lays Sol, the soil sprite from my branch on the Wishing Tree. He is glow-lost, face down on the earth, sobbing. I tune in to his emotions, but all I can see are the shadows of doubts that have crept into his thoughts and overwhelmed him with grief.

"What's the matter?" I ask, my own worries momentarily forgotten.

Sol looks up, startled, his face streaked with dirt and tears.

"Oh… it's you," he whispers, drying his eyes with his hands. "I've made a terrible mess of everything."

"What happened?"

"I helped plant a dream, but it's all gone wrong. Then, *you* caught the wish that should have been mine to resolve."

"How do you mean?"

Sol tells a long story about the dream he and his fellow sprites planted into their landowner's mind, each protecting a different form of nature on his vast estate. As he nears the end, Lydia arrives, panting.

"I tuned into your issue, Sky, and thought I might be

able to help find a solution."

"This is Sol, a soil sprite of Northumberland," I say. "Are we allowed to confer over wishes?"

"We are going to have to," Lydia replies. "Oh my goodness, Sol. You were one of the many sprites who planted the dream into Maximus's mind, weren't you?"

"That's right!" Sol exclaims, cheering slightly. "We created the dream the night before last. Max took it to heart, and the next thing we knew, he was on his way to Wonderland. Fortunately, I arrived in time to catch the wish I hoped he'd make. But Sky caught it instead."

"Everything happens for good reason," Lydia says.

"Well, here's the wish," I say, waving it apologetically. "Since you inspired Max to make it, Sol, I agree you should solve it. I have no idea of where to begin in any case."

"It's not that simple," says Sol. "The idea for the dream originated from a magazine article that caught Max's interest, but he's since set that idea aside. I wanted the dream to inspire a broader vision for Max to change farming practices, not just on his estate, but everywhere. I led the team to replenish the soil," he chokes. "I keep thinking that someone else could have done it better… It's going around and around in my head that I ruined everything and got it all wrong."

Lydia crouches beside him. "You haven't failed," she tells him. "Those whispers aren't yours, Sol. Sometimes they're seeded by the Murmurers – they prey on hopeful minds. But you did what was right; it's just not finished yet. Max's farm is a good start."

"But soil health is essential to life," says Sol. "If we don't act quickly, food will run out, and land will be washed away. Rivers polluted with chemical fertilisers don't just kill fish; they poison our food. Regenerative farming has to become the norm."

Lydia stands, brushing the soil from the hem of her skirt. "Remember what Miss Twig taught us: real change takes time because it grows roots first, deep down and out of sight, before any signs of life appear. And when doubt creeps in, when you start to hear those whispers, it often means you're closer to breaking through the surface than you think. The Murmurers don't waste their breath on lost causes, Sol. They only trouble those with real power to make a difference."

Sol stares at the ground. "I just thought I'd be better at this."

"Same," I admit, kneeling down beside him. "I understand - I really do. When that wish came hurtling towards me, I froze. I was so afraid of getting it wrong that I stopped trusting myself. I lost sight of the fact that magic isn't in knowing everything; it's about figuring out how to solve the problem."

Sol looks up, furrowing his brow. "But Max… his only focus has always been on himself."

"Even so," Lydia says, "dreams don't disappear. They

wait, like seeds in the soil."

She hands me a wish. "This one's from a young woman who wants nutritious food for everyone. She works in vintage fashion. Probably thinks it's a quick fix, but moving from one system to another can take five to ten years. She's not set up to follow it through, as Miss Twig explained she'd have to. She has neither land nor a credible voice to have a say about soil. Not yet…"

I stop in my tracks. "Wait," I say, turning toward Sol. "I've had an idea. If I tune into Max, I could shift the responsibility back to you," I assure him.

Sol blinks in surprise. "You'd do that?"

"Of course. I won't let you down. Trust me." I beckon Lydia to come with me. And for the first time in a long while, I trust myself too.

* * *

Lydia and I find Max beside the Wishing Tree. I tune into his thoughts and uncover the article Sol mentioned about regenerative agriculture, which inspired his dream. Tucked away in the back of his mind, all it needs is a gentle nudge to bring it to his attention.

A young woman in a white, embroidered cotton nightdress stands beside him. The sunlight catches her loose curls, turning them golden, reflected in the aura I notice around her delicate frame. Her kind eyes turn to him with quiet confidence, radiating an air of gentleness and elegance.

"She's the one who made the wish I caught," Lydia whispers.

Max stands tall beside her, his light hair swept back, and his usual poise softened by the moment. Something about her calm and grounded presence puts him at ease. Realising they are both dressed in nightclothes makes him feel even more comfortable. He smiles and strikes up a conversation.

"Were you caught off guard, like me, before following the rainbow?" Max boldly asks.

"Actually, no," she laughs. "I wore this nightdress on purpose as my self-expression."

"Oh," he replies. "I dressed like this on impulse," he admits, somewhat pleased that he had.

She flicks her hair back and smiles. "Well, it's all I had in stock in un-dyed cotton, simple and natural – a fashion statement to show I care about nature," she replies, her twinkling eyes helping him relax.

"That's refreshing," Max says. "Oh, my goodness!"

"What do you mean? It's not that strange, is it?"

"Sorry, no. It's quite something else that just popped into my mind. Do you know anything about regenerative farming?" he asks.

"Only a little," she says, watching a cabbage white flit across the field. "I've heard it helps the land heal, reviving soil, so it can grow healthy food, which is what interests me," she smiles.

Max nods in quick succession. "Yes, me too. I put it passed my farm manager a while back, but the idea felt too big at the time. Too risky." He hesitates. "It's hard to admit, but like so many others, I've followed the path that promises quick results. I've worked the land so hard, forgetting that soil needs a rest with a chance to recover. We did it to grow more and more, to fill supermarket shelves and meet endless demand."

The young woman listens without judgement. "It's not forgetting," she says softly. "It's surviving. Farmers have carried so much on their shoulders, but it's never too late to change."

"Klim! That's it!" Max suddenly exclaims. "The article that sparked my dream! Rebuilding the soil to attract biodiversity, stronger crops and resilience in the face of droughts and floods. It struck a chord in me, and I want to follow it up," Max says, his voice quick with anticipation.

"That sounds amazing," she says, her face lighting up with genuine encouragement.

"Klim explains how simple things like rotating crops, composting and letting the soil breathe can store carbon underground and restore balance. But the best part is that it brings life back to the fields. It's exactly what I want to do."

"I'd love to be part of that," she replies cheerfully. "I came here today from the coast to wish for a future where everyone has access to nutritiously grown food. Maybe we should join forces?"

Max nods. "Yes… maybe it was fate that sent me that invitation to come," he says, looking straight at her. "We could create a model farm, somewhere people can visit, explore and learn from. Sometimes, all it takes is witnessing change to believe it's within reach."

"That's brilliant!" she claps, bubbling with enthusiasm. "Just imagine communities not only working in harmony with nature but flourishing because of it, restoring the land and helping themselves in the process." The woman's voice grows stronger with her every word. "Regenerative farming could transform everything," she says. "Let's reach out to Klim, and to anyone else ready to make it happen."

Sol catches up with us, expressing appreciation for helping things work out.

With a spring in his step, Max extends his arm for the young woman to take. "Let's get going," he says. "I'm Max, by the way."

"Sure Max! Let's!" she grins. "I'm Valentine. Where are we headed?"

"Home," Max replies. "I've found more than just a purpose; I've found a new way of life. Will you come with me?"

"I'm with you every step of the way," she says,

without a second thought.

As they set off across the field, Max quickens his pace, feeling lighter on his feet than ever. Lydia and I watch them go, the sun warming their backs. Sol and his team follow closely behind, silent and proud.

"The magic of dreams and the wonder of wishes," I sigh, feeling a sense of achievement.

"Yes," Lydia agrees. "They're about planting seeds for the future, and there's magic in that."

As Max and Valentine disappear into the distance, I turn to Lydia. "This is far more rewarding than granting wishes with the wave of a magic wand," I say. "It's the dreams backed by effort that will shape a brave new world." I smile, filled with a quiet sense of hope. "Now, all I need do is untangle the wish I caught in the tree and head off to the Pixie Kingdom to see where other dreams might lead."

5

CALLS TO ACTION

In a quiet ground-floor living room in London, The Lady pauses. Her fingers hover above the keyboard, typing a message to the house owner in the Pixie Kingdom, confirming the guest list for the dinner they will host on Monday.

All morning, subtle impressions had brushed through her thoughts – a man standing on a balcony, awakened by a dream of wildflowers, a sense of longing, as if outdated systems were about to be replaced. She could hear a sudden swell of birdsong, feel a breeze scented with wild mint, and picture a rainbow over the landscape, accompanied by laughter that seemed to belong to another world.

The Lady had grown accustomed to these fleeting moments. She blinks once and smiles – a small, private smile, though she can't quite explain why. It is simply a feeling, as if something had shifted in the world for the better. It was as though others had truly understood the things that she, too, cared about.

* * *

Lydia and I join our team for a picnic beside the Wishing Tree, sitting on a patchwork of blankets and enjoying the warm buzz of conversation as we share news about Max and Valentine, delighting in our small victory.

"But there's more," I say, waving the unresolved wish above my head. "Anil, we need to return to the Pixie Kingdom almost immediately if I'm going to solve this one."

"What?" Anil frowns, "I don't want to leave Wonderland, Sky. Not yet. I love it here and could stay forever."

"Same," I admit, "but we have responsibilities and important work ahead." Anil scrunches her nose. "It's our test case, Anil, to know whether the dream I planted in the spring has taken root and can grow into something significant."

"But I love catching wishes," she sighs. "I think I've got a knack for it."

"I'm not suggesting we leave now," I reassure her, "and definitely not before the party this afternoon."

"Why go there at all when you can tune in from here?" she asks, with a hopeful shrug. "You've already triumphed in helping Sol with Max. Can't we use similar tactics without having to fly all that way."

"Let me sail you there," offers Pascal as he adjusts his captain's cap.

"What a great idea," I say, bolstered by his support.

"But why the rush to get to the Pixie Kingdom anyway?" asks Kobalos.

I explain my dream of the duck named Salter and the unresolved wish held in my hand.

"Let me see," says Liam, reaching for the wish.

I hand it over.

He reads it out slowly, the words weighing heavily: "'*This wish comes from a place of no return! Find a nature-based solution to cool the planet and take action. Bring temperatures down. Do not delay...*'"

"It's the reason you went to the Pixie Kingdom in the first place," Lydia says, her eyes bright. "To find an industrialist willing to make things right. I'd like to come with you this time."

"Me too," say Layla and Anito in unison.

"Perfect!" I clap my hands. "That dream I planted was meant to bring scientists, policymakers, visionaries, and industrialists together – not just to talk, but to sit side by side at the changemakers' table, as heroes of our time."

"'*Les Résolveur de Notre Temps*,'" Pascal grins. "They were mentioned on our invitation to Wonderland, along with dinners in rue Ducale."

Anil's eyes shine with quiet resolve. "Of course I'll come, Sky. It'll be fascinating - five sprites, unseen at the table, listening and observing. Tune into The Lady, she's at the heart of all this."

"I already have," I reply with a smile. "Just like my dream said, it's happening on Monday."

"Then flying makes more sense," Pascal nods. "But join us for breakfast on the boat before you set off." He turns to Liam and Kobalos. "I'll be delighted to sail us to my beloved homeland, joined by the rest of our team during the week. We'll exchange ideas at the tea party this afternoon," he adds, giving a theatrical regal wave with his hand.

"I'd give anything to sail across with you," Liam grins, already looking forward to the trip. "See you later in the storytelling garden," he says, heading off. "I've reserved your seats for teatime - don't be late."

* * *

In the early afternoon, the storytelling garden begins to come alive. Children and adults settle into clusters – some on tartan rugs, others on benches sheltered beneath a canopy of flowers, or on chairs tucked away in alcoves, protected from the wind. Birds flit from branch to branch, chattering above the gathering. Squirrels dart between picnickers, and in the undergrowth, a nursing hedgehog snuffles around in search of crumbs.

A festive hush of anticipation fills the air as tea tables

are set with delicate china and towers of scones, their home-backed aroma mingling with the scent of blossom carried by the breeze. An undulating path meanders between the trees, leading to a small, sun-dappled storytelling platform shaded by leafy branches. There, Liam stands in wait, humming an Irish jig, tapping time with his feet.

"Is the Queen of Hearts coming this afternoon?" a small, wide-eyed child asks.

"To be sure," Liam replies, brushing pollen from a stool. "Queen Titania invited her, but she's far too grand to reply. When the Queen of Hearts arrives at any of the events, you'd think she was still in charge."

"I've heard whispers," I say. "Bits and bobs about what happened between them. Do tell us the story, Liam."

Liam glances at the children laughing and playing beneath the trees. He points towards the palace: "Forewarned is forearmed," he says, observing festivity fairies and elves place canvas seats in rows. With time in hand, he gestures for us to come closer. Anil and I perch on the edge of a wicker chair beneath a broad bough, its leaves rustling as if they, too, want to hear the story.

"Long ago," Liam begins, his eyes twinkling, "at the heart of a midsummer night's dream, Queen Titania quarrelled with King Oberon and unsettled Nature herself. Flowers refused to bloom, crops failed, and the skies grew wild with storms.

Then, when Titania heard tales of Wonderland, something else was stirring to cause concern – the age of industry – loud, proud and hungry for fuel. It prompted Titania to turn her back on the mortal courts of Athens, seizing the moment to bring the light of fairyland into Wonderland and share its reign in the name of nature.

"And so it was, as her world teetered between imagination and invention, Titania followed the secret tunnel into Wonderland, not in search of power, but to safeguard the true wonder of Wonderland, protecting goodness and beauty in the material world and the delicate rhythms of nature.

"Here, she joined forces with the Queen of Hearts, and for a time, they stood side by side – two radiant rulers at the heart of a changing realm in flux. They did not seek to govern with a rod of iron, but to weave quiet magic into the seams between realms, guiding the material world, already forgetting its bond with nature beneath the shadow of rising chimneys, billowing factory smoke, and the hiss of steam.

"Titania ruled with quiet strength, listening to the whispers of rivers, the breath of the soil, the murmurs of mycelium, and the steady grounding of roots deep beneath the earth. She gave life the space to grow and bloom. Instead of forcing wonderland into rigid shapes, Queen Titania guided it with creative care, cherishing each note of its melody, ensuring that nothing was stifled or lost.

"The Queen of Hearts, in contrast, governed with fierce determination, focusing solely on a clear goal, regardless of what else might be overlooked, ignored or brushed aside. She had no patience for hesitation, for wandering thoughts; true leadership to her, meant acting swiftly and maintaining control. For a time, they ruled in harmony – like two dancers in step. Titania's wide view allowed the Queen of Hearts to step forward when sharp focus was needed, taking centre stage with certainty and command, while Titania held the balance of nature, attuned to the rhythm of their realm, cradled in the palm of her hand."

Liam shifted slightly on his stool, his eyes narrowing.

"But balance," he says, "is a tricky business. The Queen of Hearts came to believe her way was the only way, not understanding how she and Titania complemented each other. Titania captured the whole picture with empathy and imagination, much like the right side of the brain, always open to possibilities. It's how music, stories, and feelings are understood, not just as sounds or words but also as elements of something deeper that gives them meaning. But the Queen of Hearts only understood certainty, always seeking order. Much like the left side of the brain, she sought to analyse things by breaking them into parts, giving them a label, mastering them and putting them back together in a way that suited her logic that followed ideas in a straight line, even when the path called for a curve. And yet, although her way of thinking helps to focus, plan, and get things done, it needs guidance - the *left mind is a wonderful servant*, but the *right mind is the true master*. When it leads without the other, it can confuse efficiency with wisdom, and control with understanding."

A soft rustle passes through the listeners.

"Titania believed fairies should guide humanity with subtlety, gently lighting the way back to nature. But the Queen of Hearts demanded swift action – clear, bold, visible, and impossible to ignore. What began as a shared purpose slowly fractured into rival visions. Titania trusted in the natural growth of change, while the Queen of Hearts grew restless, determined to drive it by force.

"Although both sought to protect Wonderland and the world beyond, their rift deepened." Liam pauses. "Titania believes in uniting fairies and children to transform nature back to health from the wounds inflicted by the material world. But the Queen of Hearts…" he tails off for a moment. "She lost her faith in humanity, seeing them as selfish hypocrites, and sleepwalkers wandering through a world of broken promises while the earth cried out for help." He gently shakes his head. "The Queen of Hearts grew bitter, twisted with disappointment." Liam leans in slightly. "One day, she followed the secret tunnel out of Wonderland and crossed into the material world – a curious traveller, perhaps enchanted by the lure of its glitter. For a moment she hoped she might find a new kind of power there, but what she found only deepened the unrest within her."

A group of children had begun to gather. A girl with freckles and a crown of daisies sat at the foot of the platform. A boy joined her, scribbling notes, while another named Henry, who had been there from the start, edged in close, sitting cross-legged at Liam's feet, eyes wide with curiosity.

"The Queen of Hearts tried to play the material world at its own game," Liam says, his tone darkening. "She mistook control for strength and lost her compass. It hardened her heart."

He looks down, his voice gentle.

"Her mind, once alive with precision and wonder, became fixated on rules alone. This single-minded focus led her to act without feeling, make decisions without empathy, and fix things that didn't need mending. The volatile Queen of Hearts, quick to anger and action, came to believe that a swift chop was the answer to every problem. Cut off from the patience and wisdom of Titania's perspective, she lost all sense of proportion, leading even her good intentions to go terribly wrong..."

Henry leans forward, catching Liam's eye.

"She allied with the Murmurers," Liam whispers, "for what she believed was for good reason. When she returned to Wonderland, where rules shifted like smoke, a clever child named Alice questioned her. The King of Hearts… he didn't stand by the Queen, remaining silent while whispers of her being obsolete grew louder, branding her a relic, a fairy tale."

Gasps flutter through the listeners in shock.

"Bitterness gathered like storm clouds around her throne, and the Winds began to blow unease. And so," Liam continues, crouching low, "for the first time in its long history, Wonderland faced a painful choice. Queen Titania and the high sprites gathered in the palace court. With sadness, the Four Winds banished the Queen of Hearts to exile, not to punish, but to protect the realm from rigid laws that drained the wonder from Wonderland. Her courtiers, once full of spirit, grew disillusioned – reduced to cogs in a system, expected to abandon curiosity, imagination, and the freedom to choose.

"Titania, despite her compassion, feared that justice, once fair and just, had soured into something harsher - more punishing than protective. Where harmony once flourished, strict order was enforced. If allowed to continue unchecked, this would stifle the very essence that kept Wonderland alive, shifting from a delicate balance of symbiotic coexistence to the cold certainty of a mechanical system."

"But the Queen of Hearts came back…" the daisy-crowned girl whispers.

"She did," Liam nods. "Cloaked in grace and speaking the language of change, Titania welcomed her with back. Some say she glimpsed a hint of the Queen she once knew. Others believed her return was more calculated - to weave a web of quiet influence and intrigue, ensuring that should Titania ever falter, she would be ready to claim the throne in her place."

He leans forward, his voice dropping a notch. "It's said she's begun speaking to the Murmurers again. And not just them, but those who linger behind them in the shadows;

the Fogkeepers."

The word slips into the garden like a chill.

"Some say she knows who they truly serve. Others say she doesn't. But either way, her old anger has been reignited."

"Does Queen Titania know?" Henry asks with searching eyes.

Liam studies him for a moment, catching a glimmer of something deeper than curiosity – a quiet blend of wonder and an early spark of wisdom.

"She knows more than she lets on," he replies. "But Titania plays the long game. She believes that true strength lies not in punishment but in the potential for change. That even a heart twisted by pride might one day be healed.

"She stays," Liam says at last, his tone edged with pity. "In her own wing of the palace. She rarely shows herself. Somewhere inside, the Queen of Hearts still believes the world owes her devotion. Not because she wants adoration, but because control is the only thing that's never let her down. She doesn't fear being unloved, but being dismissed, made small, humiliated."

"Why?" asks the girl with daisies in her hair.

"Because humiliation cuts deeper than betrayal," Liam tells her. "The King of Hearts mocked her. Alice laughed at her. Her pride was shattered, not broken in battle, but chipped away in front of an audience. And instead of healing, she hid. What festered wasn't sorrow, it was bitterness. And that bitterness took root. Those roots… grew thorns."

A hush clings to the garden. Even the trees seem to stand still. Then, from somewhere nearby, sounds of laughter bubble up. Children settle on picnic blankets, and a rustle of activity engulfs the lawn. The spell is broken, but the echo of Liam's words lingers in the air, mingling with the scent of wild honeysuckle. As a gathering audience congregates in front of the stage, Liam adjusts the brim of his hat.

"It's an on-going story," he says softly, more to himself, "and one we'll return to another time."

Elves step onto the platform to set up an umpire's chair for Liam, providing him with a broad view of the garden. Liam takes his position, surveys the crowd, and clears his throat. Anil and I settle on a branch above. The garden shifts from hushed whispers to murmurs of wonder that ripple through the audience like a gentle breeze blowing over the long grass, expectant eyes focused on Liam.

6

THE STORYTELLING GARDEN

From his elevated seat, Liam's voice resonates with enthusiasm. "Are you sitting comfortably?" he asks, allowing the question to linger. "Many of us here today have travelled from far and wide. Would you believe it? I only arrived myself last night from Northern Ireland and spent the evening beneath the Wishing Tree – not away with the fairies, mind, but in the company of their very own Queen Titania, who will join us for tea after a tale or two."

"Ooh!" the audience gasps in playful anticipation.

"Did you happen to see the new sign at the Wishing Tree?" Liam asks, a glint in his eye. "It says, '*No more material wishes will be granted by fairy folk*'." He pauses and raises an eyebrow. "Now, what do we think of *that*?" he inquires, looking out at the crowd.

As chatter ripples through the spectators, a faint rustling can be heard behind the hedge, where two indistinct figures exchange quiet murmurs, the hoods of their cloaks covering their faces. "*No more material wishes?*" one whispers to the other. "*Isn't that a bit... ridiculous?*"

Liam forms a makeshift megaphone with his palms and calls out. "Come on then," he prompts. "How much value do you place on material possessions?" Eager hands shoot up. Liam points to a girl at the back wearing a Yellowstone sweatshirt.

"My name is Sandy, and I live a few miles from Yellowstone National Park in the United States," she replies with confidence. "I guess I've never needed much, but the things I do have matter to me - not because they are shiny or new, but because they've been with me along the way. I've a special coat that's kept me warm and weathered many a storm, and a compass my granddad gave me when I was ten. The brass is tarnished, and the glass scratched, but it still points true north," she pauses. "It was made to last and is precious to me. Granddad said it was a reminder to find my own direction and not just follow someone else's path."

She stands tall, commanding the audience's attention. "I reckon things should be made to last, not to throw away. When something is crafted with care, you not only carry the designer's story but your own."

The crowd responds with applause.

"That's nice, Sandy," Liam smiles. "Are you here on vacation?"

"Yes, with my folks," she says, gesturing towards a

group seated on a rug.

"Well, then," Liam says, turning to his listeners with theatrical flair, "we are in the storytelling garden after all, so how about a little story from Sandy here – all the way from Yellowstone, the first national park in the world?"

He beckons her forward. The crowd claps enthusiastically as she makes her way to the platform, her footsteps light on the ground.

"Hi," she begins shyly. "I'd like to share a story about something extraordinary that happened in Yellowstone before I was born. It was back in 1995."

Curious glances are exchanged among the audience. With growing confidence, Sandy awaits their full attention.

"Thanks to visionary groups that stood up for their beliefs, an experimental project was launched to restore balance to the ecosystem. Once hunted and forced out of the area, wolves were reintroduced into the park to help control the overpopulation of deer. But, no one expected the remarkable changes that followed."

I conjure up a picture of the scene as Sandy describes it. The wolves, sleek and powerful, roam across a vast expanse of mountainous terrain. Sandy pushes her dark hair behind her ears, engaging with her captivated audience.

"It all began with the wolves hunting deer. This led to a rapid decline in the deer population. The wolves also caused the remaining deer to avoid certain areas of the park where they were easy prey. In the absence of deer, those areas started to regenerate, allowing wildflowers to bloom and forests of aspen and willow trees began to flourish. That's when things really started to happen."

Liam watches Sandy, impressed by her natural storytelling ability and her skill in capturing the audience's interest with carefully chosen pauses.

"As the trees and bushes grew, more berries and bugs appeared. With this increase in food sources, various bird species began to migrate to the area. The growing tree population also attracted other wildlife. Beavers, once extinct in the region, returned, and the dams they built created habitats for otters, muskrats and reptiles.

"The wolves began preying on coyotes, which led to a rise in the populations of rabbits and mice. This shift in the ecosystem, in turn, attracted more hawks, red foxes, badgers, and weasels to the park. Even the numbers of bald eagles and ravens increased. Now, here's where it gets exciting," she says, engaging the audience with her wide brown eyes.

"The wolves altered the behaviour of the rivers. With a better balance between predator and prey, even more species began to thrive. There was less erosion due to increased vegetation, which helped stabilise the riverbanks. The channels narrowed, more pools formed, and the rivers maintained a more consistent course.

"So, the wolves not only transformed Yellowstone's great ecosystem but also changed the park's physical geography. Nature is incredible," she concludes, "and it serves as our compass to find answers to problems."

Everyone claps, and some cheer. But near the back, hidden in the shadows, a hooded figure leans towards a companion, a dry voice cutting through the applause. *"Wolves saved rivers, did they? We could spin that and turn it – only a dreamer would believe such a tall tale."* The other nods slowly, adding weight to a small crack they've found in the brilliant shine of Sandy's story.

"Thank you, Sandy," says Liam "What a wonderful tale to hear, full of hope and education from a well-managed project."

His observation prompts a man to respond.

"Excuse me," comes a voice from the back with a thoughtful tone. "I'm Rolf, a wildlife biologist," he says. "I've spent decades studying the reintroduction of wolves and moose."

The audience turns their attention to him.

"Sandy's account of Yellowstone's wolves is indeed inspiring. However, my overall experience shows that reintroduction can be unsuccessful without sufficient suitable habitat, prey availability, and enough terrain for wolves to thrive. Inbreeding between them is a concern, and human conflict poses an additional challenge."

He pauses, allowing his words to settle. "These experiences teach us that while nature has remarkable resilience, our interventions must be guided by humility and a deep understanding of ecological complexities. In leadership, as in conservation, it's not just about taking action, but ensuring that our actions are informed and considerate of the whole."

The crowd nods, reflecting on his words. Just beyond the edge of the audience, two Murmurers stand quietly beneath the shadows of a hawthorn tree. They don't interrupt. They don't need to. Every balanced argument, every question without an answer – feeds them.

Liam smiles warmly. "Thank you Rolf, for sharing your invaluable perspective. Nature indeed offers profound lessons for us all." He turns back to Sandy. "Now, since you've come to Wonderland and the world of wishes, what would your Wish of the Day be, Sandy?"

She doesn't need a moment to think. "A universal wish to be picked up by all and sundry," she says, closing her eyes and pressing her fists together. "To cool the planet, like-minded people across the world joining forces, to preserve and enrich the natural world with awareness of their impact."

A nearby sprite darts forward, catching the wish mid-air before it can drift away. With a hop and a spin, she showers Sandy with fairy dust, dividing the wish into multiple parts, which she throws to the wind like dandelion seeds. All sprites among us leap up to catch a fragment.

"Wow! I never knew you could use fairy dust like that," I whisper to Anil, slipping the universal wish up my sleeve. "Do you have any spare?"

But before she has time to answer, another wish comes hurtling through the air, heading straight for Anil and nearly knocks her sideways. With quick reflexes, she steadies herself and catches it with the technique of a skilled baseball player, reading it carefully. I stare at the orb in Anil's hand, now pulsing with an odd flicker of grey light and the faint smell of smoke.

"What's it say?" I ask, wide-eyed and curious.

Anil hesitates, glancing towards the shadows beneath the hawthorn tree, where a glimmer of doubt interrupts her thoughts. "Not now, Sky," she murmurs, shaking her head. "It's… complicated. Let's listen to the rest of the stories."

Liam's voice draws the crowd's attention. "Sandy, before you take your seat, is there anything else you'd like to share?"

"Yes – just one more thing," Sandy replies. "Tree planting is becoming hugely popular, and that's brilliant, but it's an art. It shouldn't be rushed or haphazard. I met some remarkable innovators from the Netherlands here today who are leading hedge-planting projects that support biodiversity and local ecosystems. Simon, are you here?" she calls, searching the crowd.

"Indeed, I am," comes a cheerful voice from above. We all look up, squinting into the dappled light, and there he is, perched comfortably on an overhead branch, legs swinging and a wide grin on his face.

"Hello up there," Liam calls, forming an imaginary telescope with his hands. "Come on down, Simon, as they say on the television," he jokes, beckoning him forward.

Simon leaps from the branch while agilely carrying a basket brimming with fruit.

"Good afternoon, everyone," he says, smiling broadly with bright eyes, heading for the stage. "I've brought some treats – raspberries, strawberries and nuts we've grown as part of our forest farm for you to enjoy at teatime."

As he speaks, three others join him on the stage. "May I introduce my team: Sacha, Wytze and Katja," Simon says, gesturing them forward.

They each wave, their energy radiating across the crowd.

Simon continues speaking, his tone both passionate and measured. "I come from a family of ecologists, and my wish is to unite agriculture and nature. A wish we are making into a reality together."

The crowd gives a clap of encouragement.

"My practical experience in regenerative farms in Northern Italy inspired me to pursue food forestry. Our mission is to rejuvenate degraded land and show that nature and food production can thrive together."

Sacha steps forward, his voice calm but persuasive. "Today's problem lies in the obsession with mass production and low prices, often at the expense of quality and sustainability. We envision a future where food nourishes both people and the planet."

Wytze nods. "Our edible ecosystems demonstrate how

nature and agriculture can coexist. A food forest is a layered system – trees, shrubs and ground plants all working together, parts of which provide us with food."

"Our seven years of planting hedges and borders have yielded a variety of berries, fruits, spices, nuts and herbs," Katja adds. "It's not just about food; it's about cooling the area, restoring soil, increasing biodiversity and improving water quality."

Simon smiles. "We're establishing three food forests within Lingezegen Landscape Park in Gelderland, where city, agriculture and nature meet. Local residents can harvest from one forest while the others supply shops and gourmet restaurants with unique produce like truffles."

"Food forests are more than farms," Anil whispers. "They're lifelines for the planet."

Liam raises his head, his voice jubilant. "Let's give a cheer to this spectacular team of Young Food Forest Farmers!"

"Hooray!" the crowd chants, clapping and cheering without restraint.

"*Food forests*?" murmurs a dry voice near the hedgerow. "*Romantic, but try feeding a city that way.*" The words don't travel far, but just enough to be caught by a few uncertain ears.

All of a sudden, a fanfare of trumpets silences the applause. Eyes instantly turn to the path as Queen Titania appears, petalbright, her gown shimmering like morning dew on a silken web. Every step she takes seems to breathe life into the earth beneath her feet. Leaving a glow in her wake, fairies flutter about her, scattering sparkling fairy dust as they form a procession around her.

"Such rizz," whispers Anil as the Queen takes her seat at the high table.

"Let the tea begin," announces the Queen, her voice reminiscent of silver chimes.

Guests settle at trestle tables laden with cakes, wobbly jellies, and fruit punch. Food fairies flit between them, balancing trays of delicious treats. Liam hosts Simon's team at one table, while Anil and I take our seats at Queen Titania's.

The fanfare begins again, louder this time, bursting forth with pomp and ceremony as the Queen of Hearts sweeps into the storytelling garden, flanked by a flurry of courtiers, knaves, and the King of Hearts – trailing behind like a threadbare card, long worn down from being played too often and trumped too much. She raises her chin proudly at the sight of Queen Titania, her shoulders stiff and nostrils flaring, revealing a hint of old rivalry beneath her regal facade.

Queen Titania, unfazed, offers a gracious nod before turning to me with unperturbed bright eyes.

"Sky," she says, calm and confident, "Liam tells me you'll soon leave Wonderland for the Pixie Kingdom."

"Yes, ma'am," I reply. "I'm going to follow up on the dream I planted in the changemaker's mind."

"Then help it flourish," she says with a smile. "Never forget that human actions shape the world, for better or for worse. Keep that wish tucked up your sleeve as a reminder of the bigger picture and the wider purpose we share."

A knave from the Queen of Hearts' court approaches our table, his eyes lingering on the jam tarts. I watch him with suspicion, wary of his reputation for stealing them. Instead, he bows low and presents a folded note to Queen Titania, waiting silently for her response.

"Please inform Her Majesty," Titania says with a serene smile, "that I will gladly meet her in her quarters after supper this evening to discuss the rule of our realm."

She selects the finest plate of jam tarts from the table and offers it to the knave to take back to his table. As the knave retreats with his treasure, something stirs. A strange draught sweeps through the air, and the leaves at the edge of the lawn flutter against the eerie current, as if somewhere, just out of sight, someone is watching.

7

THE MURMURERS MOVE IN

The northern entrance to the palace where the Queen of Hearts resides felt colder - not just in temperature, but in atmosphere. This side of Wonderland turns away from the sun, leaning instead into the restless winds that blow without warmth. The moon hung low and watchful, casting a pale light over the stone walls, where ivy clung tightly with a relentless grip. Shadows pooled in the corners, and the hedges, once ornamental, were clipped too sharply, their bare twigs shaped in haste and anger.

We follow the moss-lined path in silence, unsure of what to expect. With every step, the air feels heavier, charged with that quiet, electric stillness that comes before a storm. Anil and I share a silent unease, a protective instinct that simmers beneath the surface as we seek to shield our Queen. But we know her to be resilient and clever. Tonight, our task is to listen and to witness the inner workings of Wonderland before our departure at first light.

We slip through an open window into the stark dining hall, greeted by the hollow echo of distant footsteps. Fairies with solemn expressions usher us to an observation gallery set on high beams, giving us a bird's-eye view of the room.

The Queen of Hearts is already present, sitting rigidly on a throne-like chair at the head of a long table, robed in blood-red velvet. She doesn't seem to notice our arrival, or if she does, she gives no sign of recognition. Her face is a mask – imperious and unreadable. She is notorious for her temper, but in silence holds something even more unsettling. When she rages, at least you know where you stand; when she is quiet, no one can be sure of what she is plotting.

Below us, the Queen rises restlessly and walks around the room. Her courtiers follow her back to the table, careful to match her pace and keep their eyes to the ground. Anil tightens her grip on my hand.

From the far end of the courtyard, a breath of jasmine wafts on the wind, a scent as distinct as a signature, heralding the arrival of Queen Titania. Dressed in a silk organza, petals float gently in her wake. Guided by a courtier, she moves confidently to the opposite end of the table and settles down with quiet, unwavering grace.

The Queen of Hearts inclines her head. "Thank you for coming," she says, her smile as sharp as a guillotine. A solemn hush envelops the chamber. Her gaze locks onto Titania with the precision of a hawk. "Tell me," she begins, her voice echoing across the marble hall. "How long will you twiddle your thumbs and pirouette in pixie circles while the material world drowns in its own folly?"

Titania does not flinch. "We do not ignore," she says calmly. "We inspire. We uplift. We remind humanity that the responsibility is theirs."

"Uplift?" scoffs the Queen of Hearts. "While the world sinks like a lead balloon? How delightfully daft!"

Titania maintains her composure. "We offer truth, hope and inspiration."

The Queen of Hearts leans forward, her eyes blazing with intensity. "Hope without resilience is a jelly without a mould! And truth – bah! Truth is whatever nonsense people prefer to believe! It's no more than a slippery eel, wriggling into whatever shape suits the teller. But fret not, dear Titania," she adds with mock brightness. "When you fail and your dreams deflate, I'll be ready – with my trusty axe of order and a rulebook thicker than a toad's tailcoat."

Winds meander through the open arches of the palace, eavesdropping. The sky dims into twilight. Titania rises gracefully. "My realm is founded on truth. Lies have no soil here in which to root. Perhaps your exile has clouded your vision," she replies.

The Queen of Hearts grunts. "Nonsense! I was exiled not for speaking falsehoods but for revealing truths uttered too soon. While you sprinkle fairy dust, I brandish facts through hoops like a flamingo in a croquet match. Now I see clear as crystal and clearer than a diamond in vinegar."

"And what do you see?" Titania inquires softly.

The Queen of Hearts stands, her hands firmly planted on the table. "A world teetering on the edge, lacking discipline and drowning in misguided do-goodism. Humanity needs a firm hand, clear rules, and decisive actions! Tension and stress are the tools of progress, my dear. Without friction, how will they adapt to the storms ahead?"

"I do not disagree," Queen Titania says gently. "*Children* are the hope. They are resilient, while grown-ups have forgotten how to listen or take action. We hear the Earth crying out, pushed past her limits – the forests withering, the oceans raging, and the mountains groaning with grief. The birds, insects, and flowers slip away like dreams, becoming extinct. Yet still, they delay."

The Queen of Hearts sweeps forward to interrupt, her gown trailing across the floor. "Dreams!" she spits. "You live in a candy-floss world, Titania. But let us not pretend, the real culprit in the material world is greed!" All eyes turn to her. "Men in smoky towers," she sneers, "plotting their fortunes. They poison the rivers and tear up the earth, then jet off to 'net zero' conferences to pat themselves on the back for doing absolutely nothing! And when I cried out for justice in the material world – for heads to roll, just like with Alice and the King - they jeered, ridiculed me, and laughed. They called *me* mad!" Her voice rings out. "I wasn't calling for madness. I was calling for *sense*! For courts that work, for rulers who actually rule! Instead, we got administrators – paper-pushers! Cowards! And you," she points at Titania, "think a daisy chain will mend a broken sky!" She lets out a cruel and bitter laugh. "They've built a fortress of denial. The Barons of Barrels, those oily buffoons – smiling at every summit while funding the death of truth! The Duke of Distraction – tearing up treaties and chuckling as the ice melts! You'll never win against them," she hisses.

"And yet," says Queen Titania quietly, "here you are – back from exile, seated at the very table you once scorned. You swore an oath to serve the realm of the living, and all I see is the loss of hope, bitterness and despair."

"I was banished for saying the truth before its time!" she snaps. "For refusing to wrap reality in fairy dust, as you tend to do. I gave you thunder and facts! Tell me, why should humanity get another chance? They've squandered every opportunity they've had! What if they don't deserve another chance?" she demands, her voice bouncing off the stone columns.

"I speak," says Titania firmly, "for the children who can still imagine the world as it could be. How it *will* be."

The Queen of Hearts turns away sharply. Down a side aisle, a chill creeps in, and with it, soft hissing whispers that begin to swirl and slither through the arches and across the hall. The Murmurers, cloaked in grey with faces hidden behind dark veils, assemble, bowing low to the Queen of Hearts. Their voices, barely audible, weave confusion. Heavy damp breaths, sighs of despondency, thread through the air as they seek victims to dampen down and thwart ideas.

"Beware the Murmurers," warns Titania. "They serve not themselves, but the Fogkeepers, masters of doubt and distraction. They sow uncertainty and halt action by drowning it in noise."

"Afraid they'll unravel your tapestry of dreams, are you?" the Queen taunts. "Spoiling your pretty plans by spinning truth into nonsense?"

"They serve the Lords of Delay and the Lords of Prevarication," Titania replies, her voice ringing clear. "They confuse, distract and divide."

The whole hall holds its breath.

Anil whispers, "The Murmurers are everywhere in Wonderland, creeping into dreams, twisting thoughts, sewing seeds of hesitation and fear."

"They sing lullabies of denial and lies," I add. "They mix everything up and call global warming a hoax."

Across the room, a Murmurer speaks in a hushed tone, chillingly audible for anyone to hear. "*No one can be sure… Perhaps it's not that bad… What's the rush?*"

"They are everywhere," I say. "Not just in Wonderland. We cannot silence them, but we can outshine them. Truth burns brighter than fog if enough voices join together, especially the young."

"The battle has only just begun," declares the Queen

of Hearts, turning away, her gown sweeping dust into the air.

"Your battles are with yourself," Titania responds. "That fire within you could illuminate the world, if only you'd let it."

But the Queen of Hearts is already out of sight, lacking the patience to hear more, let alone listen.

* * *

Anil and I tune into The Lady before settling down for the night. We find her lying quietly on her bed, gazing at the ceiling, searching for answers. Her mind swirls with thoughts – quick, sharp exchanges that flicker like fireflies in the dark. At the centre, her fears hum with the energy of unresolved anxiety. No tears, and nothing out of control – just thoughts circling around and around like birds of prey.

All of a sudden, carried on a swift gust from nowhere, a shimmering orb of light comes rushing towards me.

"Look out!" Anil shouts, ducking her head, jolting me so hard that I lose my connection to The Lady.

My instinct kicks in, and I catch the glowing ball without hesitation, losing my balance and falling backwards from the force. The wind whistles and the air crackles around me.

"It must be important," says Anil, helping me to my feet. "Go on, read it out!"

I cradle the wish carefully, feeling the warmth of its

message. "It's from The Lady," I say in amazement. "It's the same as Sandy's, the one that Queen Titania said I should keep up my sleeve – to cool the planet, like-minded people across the world joining forces – but there's a twist."

"What twist," Anil asks.

"The Lady is wishing to empower children to preserve and enrich nature, championing ideas for a sustainable world," I gasp. "She realises that children hold the key."

Anil examines the orb's particles. "Hmm," she says thoughtfully. "It's a special delivery kind of wish. The Winds of Change brought it to us with another message of their own… They've offered to guide us to the Pixie Kingdom in the morning to arrive in time to join The Lady at the offices of an insurance man."

"Hmm," I mumble, remembering my dream and the duck named Salter. "I'll start packing and will notify the others. Gather all the fairy dust you can find, Anil – it'll be handy to have. I'll let Robbie know we'll need him to double-up as our guide and as a reliable news reporter to cover the story as it unfolds."

With plans set in motion, I shift my focus back to The Lady. As she sleeps, her dream gains momentum. The Winds carry her hopes for change across the skies, weaving threads of magic into the fabric of her thoughts.

* * *

Crossing the quiet courtyard bathed in moonlight, the Queen of Hearts slips into her secret garden. Rose thorns twist up crumbling follies, and the sweet cloying scent of their dark red flowers clings to the night. She moves beneath the bridge to wait beside the hidden entrance to Wonderland. Her red silk scarf flutters in the breeze like a warning flag against the silvery darkness. A figure emerges from the shadowed tunnel that connects her kingdom to the material world, his hood drawn low, concealing all but the faint stir of his murmurs beneath it.

"How did the performance go, your Majesty?" asks the Murmurer, bowing low.

"A roaring success!" The Queen of Hearts cackles. "Titania believes I'm a wrinkled handkerchief of despair. *Despair!*" She throws her arms wide, nearly hitting the Murmurer on the nose. "Piffle and poppycock! It's not despair she should fear – it's children filled with doubt. Because once they begin to question her soft little truths, it all falls apart like spun sugar in the rain.

"Titania, dear, gentle Titania," she says, shaking her head, a crooked smile spread across her face, "has wagered her hopes on children, bless their cotton socks. But she forgets that doubt can slip in quicker than a weasel at a picnic. And she underestimates the power of a well-planted whisper of doubt."

The Murmurer listens closely.

"She sings of harmony, but doesn't dare name the real poison in the well – greed. Titania wants to uplift. I want to expose. There's power in showing the children what the grown-ups are too scared to admit."

She leans forward now, lips curling into a grin. "So plant the whispers. Twist the roots. Make them wonder if they've been fed fairy tales instead of facts. Doubt, my dear Murmurer, is more contagious than any spell ever cast, which, of course, is where you come in."

"Ah yes, doubt is our specialty," purrs the Murmurer.

The Queen twirls the end of her scarf around a finger. "Whispers, denials, distractions - a garland of headlines trimmed, snipped and spun with surgical precision! I count on you to scatter confusion like confetti at a wedding. Titania may be Queen of the Fairies," she declares, drawing herself up, "but *I* am the Queen of Hearts. And I shall prance and pirouette across the material world until it lies dizzy at my feet!"

She snaps her fingers. "The old tricks are sprouting marvellously - a puff of false balance here, a nibble of denial there – the banquet of befuddlement is in full swing."

"I fed the Lords of Delay and Prevarication," says the Murmurer with glee, "and their faithful followers with the usual lines, claiming global warming will be mild, or even beneficial."

"And do they swallow it?"

"Enough do," the Murmurer croons, dragging the words like treacle. "They bury their heads like ostriches in the sand, cheered on by the Merchants of Doubt – funded, of course, by the golden web of fossil fortune. We know the game," he adds smugly. "Create just enough confusion to halt action…"

"No!" the Queen shouts, raising her hand sharply.

"You misunderstand," she hisses, stamping her foot like a thunderclap. "That's a dull, dusty game! I want *uproar*! Confusion isn't the goal, it's the spark that starts the fire!"

The Murmurer blinks, unsure.

The Queen's eyes gleam. "We set illusions on fire. We twist the truth not to stop the world, but to *shake it awake.* Let the lies grow so loud, so foolish, that even the sleepwalkers notice." She leans in, her voice low and electric. "Let their faith in fairy tales burn to ash. Then – *then* - they will cry out for something firm. Something clear. Something strong. And I shall give it to them."

Victory rang in her voice, bold and unrepentant, yet beneath it, something restless stirred. A shadow clung to her triumph, quiet and unresolved. She began to pace again, slower this time, like a queen walking a line between conquest and regret.

"You see," she says more quietly, "when you've

watched hope crumble enough times, you stop believing in soft landings. The world is greedy and selfish, always wanting more. Chaos is necessary to smash out-dated systems for bright new beginnings – it's the broom that sweeps away the old mess. Only when the floorboards are bare can I lay down something solid: my rules, my truth, and my order. No more dreams or fluttering hopes," she sneers. "No more inconvenient questions - just discipline, direction… and me at the helm. So let there be collapse; let them fall. It's what has to be before someone is brave enough to dare to build something better."

The Murmurer tilts his head. "You mean *you*, Your Majesty?"

The Queen does not answer at once. For a flicker of a moment, her grimace falters – a cloud passing across the moon – then it returns, wider and wilder than before. Her voice, when it returns, is bright again almost too bright. "I mean whoever has the crown when the dust settles."

Their words are whisked away on the wind, carried across the palace roof – deceit dressed as logic, truth buried in riddles beneath opinion. They slip back into the shadows. But high above, the Winds of Change catch their vibrations, carrying them to Titania, Queen of the Fairies, stirring her into fretful, restless wakefulness.

* * *

As the palace clock struck midnight, the night wrapped the landscape in a silvery hush. Lantern moths flitted lazily among the tree branches, casting soft pools of light that danced across the moss. The laughter of the day had long faded into whispers, and the children were fast asleep when an unexpected call echoed through the skies.

Charged with urgency, Queen Titania summoned sprites to join her. One by one, we appeared in answer, Anil and I eager to hear what it was she had to say.

Queen Titania, glowing faintly in the moonlight, steps forward and gestures us to form a loose semi-circle around her. Some sit cross-legged, others perch on mossy stones.

"A shadow has entered my thoughts and the court," she says. "The Queen of Hearts is causing havoc, working with deception."

A ripple of unease passes through us. I glance at Anil.

"She has found allies in the material world. Murmurers who wrap truth in riddles, who sell confusion as debate, and call care for the Earth a *luxury* – or worse, a *lie*."

The Queen kneels down, eye-level, her gaze clear. "But this is not a tale of doom. It is the moment in every story when the heroes awaken. That's you and you and you!" she says pointing each of us out. "You must carry the flame of clarity into the material world where fog has been spread. Not with anger, but with *imagination*. Not with shouting, but with *story*. Let them try to spin confusion. You shall speak through the dreams of children, reaching their unclouded hearts."

"How can we explain these lies through dreams? They're just children and don't understand the power of media, money… or the loud voices, because they haven't heard them yet," one of us asks.

"They have something far more powerful: *truth*," Titania responds. "It's what the Queen of Hearts is playing with. Let them dream about our nature summits, about the Four Winds and what humankind has inflicted on them. Let them dream about telling the stories in the school halls, let them stand on a stage and explain it in their own words. Let their laughter be louder than fear, their questions stronger than denial, and their reasoning more profound than the murmurings that spread doubt."

Queen Titania comes closer. "Let them use their gifts and talents like magic. Awaken them to the beauty of life, animating their abilities to communicate it to others. Build bridges with children everywhere, channels between the world of fairies and children. May the gift of joy prevail over despair and hope shine brighter than doubt."

We gently flap our wings in agreement.

"Let the stories flow like water, carrying the seeds of awakening to every corner of the world, adapting to any situation. Like a river, carving a path through any obstacle – strong, but gentle enough to nourish and support life."

She straightens, her expression growing resolute. "Do

not argue with the Murmurers. Tell your truth. Show them trees blooming in the desert. Show them where children plant food forests with their own hands. Show them where exhausted land can revive. Let your actions be louder than any misinformation."

The grove falls silent, save for the sound of a wind rising in the east. The wind lifts her voice and carries her message to reach those willing to listen.

"I will walk with you in your dreams, and the Winds of Change will be listening and sharing their own stories," she says softly. "Now, off you go and tell the children the stories that cannot be silenced."

As the swirling Winds of Change send Queen Titania's message through the trees, over moonlit hills and down dales, they soar to view the world from a higher vantage point, seeking new ways of seeing with a wider perspective. Each gust represents a shift in key, a change in tempo, and a redirection of possibility, attuned to the quiet command of the Queen. From their broader outlook, they see that the world around them is in flux – rivers running dry in places where children once splashed and played, forests shrinking into memory, and skies dulled by a haze not of weather but of warning. They pass over cities buzzing with urgency, where too many hurry on without looking up, and coastlines where the sea has crept too far into lives it never meant to claim. Fields once lush with promise now crack beneath the sun, while in other corners, wildflowers bloom in unexpected places as small havens of hope.

The Winds feel the pull of change everywhere, in the courage of those who dare to act and in the stillness of those who don't yet know how. Noticing a lone seed floating gently in the air, light as a whisper, full of unspoken potential, they lift it into their care. Turning eastward, they carry it on the breeze, heading towards Egypt and Kenya, lands where ancient wisdom meets youthful determination and the story of renewal that is still being written.

8

MAGIC IN THE MAKING

"Are you awake, Sky?" Anil asks, restlessly tossing and turning in bed.

"Yes. I'm thinking."

"What about?"

"Queen Titania, the Murmurers, the Pixie Kingdom, The Lady and her wish. The Food Forest folk, Max and Valentine and the dream Sol planted… I'm far too excited to sleep."

"Same, but I've something else I have to do."

"How do you mean?" I ask with surprise.

"The wish I caught in the storytelling garden," Anil says.

"Shook! With all that's been going on, I nearly forgot about it. Is there anything I can do to help?"

"I hope so."

"Pass it over."

Anil fumbles around in the bedside drawer.

"It's a wish to re-green parched, dry land." Anil says, shaking it open and reading through the text. "*Restoring habitats and providing grass for cattle to graze so tribespeople can farm again,*" she looks up, "*growing food for thousands of locals in Africa, as they once did.*"

"Deserts becoming lush… that's fantastical!"

"I know, and it's thrown me into turmoil. How can I help bring about the impossible, Sky, without magic?"

I lie on my bed, gazing out at the Wishing Tree, willing it to help us find an answer. A rare tear rolls down my cheek onto my pillow, and with it, I pick up a thought.

"Hey," I say, leaning over and pulling at Anil's sleeve. "Wait a minute. The wish made by Sandy, said for *like-minded people across the world to join forces to preserve and enrich the natural world.* Think about it – not only is it no different to The Lady's, but almost identical to the wish I read at the Temple of the Four Winds to *unite nations through the love of nature* – remember?"

"What of it?" Anil asks, sitting up and rubbing her eyes.

"Something is telling us to join hands as *one* nation of the world, striving to protect our '*mother*' - Earth!"

"That sounds right," Anil says.

"Well, it's sparked a memory. The sprites that spoke at the Nature Summit - a desert sand sprite from the Middle East said she'd found a way to create an oasis in the heat of Kuwait, remember? So it *is* possible!"

"You're right, Sky. She planted trees," Anil says. "There was another story, too, from a sprite living in Africa near the Sahara desert. He said he had to work at night and sleep during the day to avoid the heat and would have to migrate."

"Both said temperatures were reaching fifty degrees centigrade where they came from, the hottest they'd ever known. More and more of the land is drying out and becoming desert, causing temperatures to rise further."

"But she planted trees on a patch of desert near a motorway."

"Yes, even though many said it was impossible to plant anything in the sand because temperatures were too high, but she brought water in tanks, and her trees proved it could be done."

"She wasn't overcome by doubt. Trees provide shade that can reduce the temperature by many degrees and clean up the air in the process. The tree planter was determined," I say.

"And trees fend off dust and pollution. Remember how she told us hedgehogs and spiny-tailed lizards visit her oasis to find fresh water and shade?"

"I do. She called upon us to help make a large-scale green belt in the desert sand."

"It gives me hope, but I still don't know what to do, Sky," Anil says, despondent. "How I wish I could help those suffering from draught to cultivate fertile land, but I can't see the path."

"Wait a minute," I say as a vision pops to the forefront of my mind. I turn to Anil with a quiet smile. "She's begun. The Lady, I mean."

"Begun what?"

I concentrate hard. "Queen Titania had a hand in it!"

"A hand in what?"

"In planting a vivid dream about the Nature Summit, and the rainbows uniting nations through the love of nature. The Lady wants to do just that."

"I don't get it. What's the relevance?"

"The dream has inspired The Lady to work with schools, encouraging children to develop creative skills connecting to nature, finding purpose in helping each other." I close my eyes and pick up The Lady's thoughts. "They'll tell their stories in pictures, on stages, dramatise reality to grown-up audiences and become leaders in their own right." I look out of the window with wonder at the Wishing Tree. "Queen Titania," I whisper, "has begun a new dream of hope."

Overtaken by tiredness, we are unaware that the Winds of Change hover around us after a long and eventful journey, tuning into opportunities and collecting stories to help the Four Winds from losing control of the weather, restoring natural harmony to life on Earth.

* * *

That afternoon, in the hush of her study, The Lady sets down her pen. Something is stirring that can't be explained with logic, schedules or policy briefs. It comes from a deeper place – a whispering current of knowing that she had learned to instinctively trust long ago.

She closes her eyes and sits very still.

All morning, something stirred at the edges of her awareness – impressions without form, like forgotten dreams rising in vague memory. Not thoughts exactly, but sensations, nudging her towards something she couldn't quite grasp. A sense that somewhere, beyond the veil of what people referred to as 'real life', something was urging her to take action. She didn't consciously recognise where her ideas came from, only that they were arriving with increasing clarity. Not with the weight of logic, but with the lightness of knowledge.

Seeing us in Queen Titania's dream had stirred the child within her, eager to explore, learn and grow. She saw that where the Murmurers brought fog and confusion, we bring clarity. Not through argument or persuasion, but by awakening what is already within us – the inner child who sees through nonsense, not as mere spectators, but as creators with the power to transform our realities. In this light, adults remember how to care, how to imagine, and how to put the future first. They come to understand that it is not naïve to seek a better way of living, but is essential if we are to thrive without destroying the world that sustains us.

The Lady rises and crosses the room to the window, drawn by a feeling. The clouds are moving fast, restless, as if something in the upper air has been stirred awake, gathering momentum with a mind of its own. There had been unsettling signs for weeks - flash floods tearing through cities with sudden fury, rivers swelling, rising in revolt, wildfires crackling across dry hills. It was as if nature demanded attention and the skies cried out for help. Was it merely the weather rebelling, or had the planet itself, at last, found its voice to speak loud enough to be heard? The thought drifts through The Lady's mind. It echoes like a memory from childhood, not in words, but a feeling close to her heart…

And then she remembers her dream – the one where the Four Winds themselves had gathered, alive and restless, holding council at their Temple of the Four Winds in Yorkshire. Yes, The Lady thought, - a nature summit called by Titania, Queen of the Fairies. Not one filled with pomp and long speeches. Not with rows of delegates or observers scribbling notes, but something else: A bridge that lay between the hard edges of climate change and the soft, bright fantasy world of children and fairies. A place where a *voice* was given to sprites to tell their truth in a way adults had forgotten how to, and saying it so people would listen and understand.

Yes. That was it. The story is all in her head now, ready to write down. The Lady steps back from the window, her eyes suddenly bright. She reaches for a fresh sheet of paper, her fingers trembling at the challenge – not from fear, but from urgency. She picks up her pen.

"Let this be their voice," she murmurs.

And far above, riding on the high thermals of communication, I feel it – a shift in the air, a thread woven through a dream into a deed.

* * *

The Winds of Change sweep boldly across the deserts of Egypt, dancing above rippling dunes, winding their way past crumbling temples, through the stillness of the Sahara and over arid lands etched with ancient stories. They whistle through date palms and olive groves, gathering tales and carrying fragments of wonder. Southward, they pass over acacia trees and herds of gazelle, weaving through dry riverbeds and over valleys where elephants had once wandered freely. In Kenya, they soar above vibrant markets, their colours fluttering like flags in the wind, and over quiet classrooms, where the sound of nature's revival echoes in children's voices. Small hands plant seeds with big dreams, and laughter floats on the breeze alongside songs of change.

Filled with all they have seen and heard, the Winds of Change turn homeward, eager to carry their discoveries into the world of dreams.

By nightfall, they reach Wonderland. They circle around the Wishing Tree before slipping into our lodgings through an open window. Spinning around us, we're overwhelmed by a sense of sleep, the room cooled to stillness. Our eyelids close, soothed into a tranquil moment and the promise of a bedtime story.

"Far, far away," one of the Winds begins, "in the global South," whispers another. "Dennis and Peter," adds a third, "two friends from Amsterdam, stood among a group of farmers in Africa. In the heat of the day, Dennis and Peter shared their vision to evergreen the landscape to help the planet heal, creating thriving communities across Africa over the next ten years.

"'We'll inspire people everywhere to join in our mission,' Peter said. 'We'll use nature's own tools to assist us. Plants and trees are the planet's air conditioners – they remove carbon from the atmosphere, cool the land, and make everything around them healthier.'

"'We need to act together and we need to act fast,' Dennis urged.

"One of the farmers nodded, wiping his brow. 'When we care for the land, it cares for us. Restoring the soil brings back water, brings back food, supports wildlife and builds a better future for all.'

"'Precisely,' Dennis replied, sweat trickling beneath the brim of his wide straw hat. 'A greener planet is about teamwork – nature helping us, and us helping nature, giving and receiving so everything can grow stronger together. We'll restore degraded land, restore water and food security, biodiversity, and the quality of life for millions of people and animals.'

"'Yes,' said Peter, "it's about restoring balance – allowing each element of nature to work hard, helping themselves and each other.'

"Suddenly, the dream shifts. I find myself hovering above an Egyptian desert. In the distance, a man goads cattle across the sands, spreading their dung. He wears a T-shirt that reads, 'Subsidies cut for basic foodstuff inspiring the Sekem Initiative'.

A gentle wind whispers his name: Dr Ibrahim Abouleish. "He stands beside a simple white building on seventy hectares of once barren desert northeast of Cairo. His wife and young son stand beside him. And around them, the impossible has happened. The scene before them represents not just the future but also the present day. In stark contrast to the arid surroundings, the landscape of today is alive, green, generous and thriving." The voice of the wind tells me that Ibrahim employed biodynamic agricultural methods to revive the desert, but he hasn't just grown crops – he has cultivated a community.

I feel uplifted, buoyed by the beauty of human hands

working with nature rather than against it. His dream had come true. And now, it is part of mine.

I fall asleep happy.

In the morning, I compare my dream with Anil.

"Same!" Anil interrupts before I can finish. "And told by the Winds of Change, no less. Pascal says when the winds shift, they change the circumstances around you."

"I know," I wink. "With time to adjust your sails, … steering to new horizons."

"There's something odd going on, Sky," says Anil. "We must have tuned into the same vibes by trying to understand how to turn deserts into lush land."

"Defo," I agree.

Anil pauses. "What do you think Dr Abouleish's T-shirt meant?"

"I traced the scene back in my mind this morning. It was in the 1970s, when Ibrahim was a young father," I say.

Anil raises an eyebrow.

"A time when many governments, including Egypt, cut subsidies to farmers for producing basic foods like bread and rice," I explain. "Families couldn't pay for what they used to be able to afford. It pushed Abouleish to find a way to solve the problem and feed his family."

"So the struggle made him act?"

"Yes. He adapted to tough times, and he didn't give up. That's the part that matters." I glance at Anil. "Even though a part of me longs for a shortcut, a wand, anything to fix things without the waiting, our dreams show that magic is everywhere, waiting to be found – people across the world working together, turning deserts into gardens."

We exchange a smile, feeling a sudden wave of satisfaction. Then, a bird calls sharply from the rooftop. Anil sits up straight. "The sun's already up!"

We look at each other – wide-eyed.

"Our bags!"

In a flurry of limbs and laughter, we scramble into our clothes. "Pascal will be waiting," I say, half-laughing, half-panicked.

"Breakfast on the boat," Anil grins, pulling her cap down.

"Then… the Pixie Kingdom," we say with sudden excitement, strapping on our knapsacks

Before leaving, we pause at the doorway of our little room and look out at the Wishing Tree for the last time. With a sudden whoosh, it waves us goodbye.

9

THE WINDS OF CHANGE

In time for breakfast, the morning sun sparkles like magic across the marina.

"Hello," Pascal calls with a wave from the cockpit, leaping to his feet. "Such a pity you won't be sailing with us this time," he says with a bow as we step aboard to the smell of home baked bread. "Do make yourselves at home."

Lydia, Layla and Anito wave from the table. Kobalos is deep in a book, his brow furrowed in concentration. He looks up and smiles.

"How are you getting along with the wonder of wishes?" he asks.

"I'm glad you asked that," says Anil. "I've caught a stubborn one. It felt impossible yesterday. Hopeless, even… until Sky remembered the stories from the nature summit."

"Ah, yes," Pascal nods. "Ice melting and sprites

melting too, I seem to remember."

"But last night, Sky and I dreamt of desert sand brought back to life, and Africa made lush and green."

"Aha! Like the tree planter told us," Kobalos says, thinking back.

"Africa, you say?" Liam calls, emerging from the kitchen with a tray of fresh bread and leftover cakes and biscuits from yesterday's tea. "I stumbled upon an article that might help with that wish of yours," he says, placing the tray on the table and darting off to fetch it from his cabin. Moments later, Liam returns with a magazine under his arm, a plate of ginger biscuits in one hand and a bowl of sugar lumps in the other.

"It's an interview with Dennis Karpes and Peter Westerveld, founders of *Justdiggit,"* he says. "Guess where they're from and I'll give you an extra biscuit," he says, placing them on the table.

Anil and I exchange glances.

"Amsterdam. It's in The Netherlands," we answer in unison.

"Ha!" Liam claps in amazement. "Pascal is sailing us there next week to drop off Katja and the boys and to meet up with you. In the meantime, listen to what these guys are doing. It's something incredible that could help make that wish you caught come true."

He flips open the magazine. Anil closes her eyes, lying

back to listen.

"'In our projects, we work with communities and local partners to regreen dry land. We dig bunds – curved trenches that harvest rainwater – revive trees, and create seed banks. With patience, even long-dormant seeds can begin to grow again,'" Liam reads, looking up with excitement. "And the best part? The people living there run the entire operation themselves."

"Hold on a minute," Anil says, sitting up. "How do bunds work?"

"I'll try to explain," Liam replies, grabbing a few circular biscuits. He breaks them in half and props them up with sugar lumps on the tray. "Bunds are semi-circular mounds of earth, like this. They're angled to trap rainwater that would otherwise run off and be wasted."

"Like desert fairy circles?" Lydia asks, intrigued.

"I'd say so," Pascal nods. "I've seen them in the dry grasslands of Namibia. Some believe they bring good luck to fairy villages hidden underground, but they're more likely the clever work of sand termites, nature's secret gardeners." Pascal picks circular biscuits from the plate and arranges them in a honeycomb shape on the table. "Imagine this: wide circles across parched land, four to ten meters in diameter. Rainwater seeps in and stays there, allowing grass to grow around the edges. The termites feed on the grass and gradually widen the ring. They can store more water, thanks to these tiny soil engineers."

I lean forward. "I never imagined that termites could be so… heroic."

"Productive like beavers," adds Anil.

"Both work with water," Pascal agrees. "Beavers create ponds, while termites enrich the soil. Nature, when left to its own devices, always finds a way to survive."

"And so can people," Kobalos adds with kind eyes. "Humans can be powerful ecosystem engineers when they choose to be." He pauses. "Rather than struggling with wishes, why not inspire human imagination to lead the way? They are remarkable when they put their minds to it."

I smile. "Like showing children how bunds work – how they stop water from running away and bring the land back to life. That would be awesome."

Kobalos chuckles. "When I visited you in Cabilla, Sky, Merlin told me about his *Thousand Year Project.* He's working to protect and restore Celtic temperate rainforests anywhere they still exist."

I feel warm pride in my chest. "He's also leading the rewilding of our ancient woodland. Bringing back lost species and reawakening the native temperate rainforest that Cabilla once was."

"It's marvellous," Kobalos says. "But it's not a quick fix. It's a thousand-year promise. Merlin says it's about learning to think like a forest – slow, wise, and deeply connecting to everything around it."

"That's beautiful," Anil murmurs, her voice quiet.

We sit in silence. Around us, the breeze carries the scent of moss and pine.

A thousand years, I think. We need to find something quicker.

"He believes if we act now with enough humility," Kobalos adds, "the land itself will respond. By healing the rainforest, humanity will also heal something within themselves."

"Yes," says Liam. "Long before people arrived on the scene, vast parts of the Earth were shaped by wind, water, fire and ice. In some places, the rainfall was more frequent. Seeds drifted on the breeze or clung to the feathers of birds. Life took hold, and trees began to grow, slowly at first, then in thickets and towering canopies, layer upon layer. The trees attracted more rain, and the rain encouraged more life. Over thousands of years, forests formed clouds, and clouds formed weather. The rainforest developed into its own unique ecosystem."

Kobalos nods. "A reminder of time and balance - the lungs of the Earth. Once destroyed, they don't easily return."

Anito bows with respect. "We must nurture ideas for long-term benefit because we need to believe in the future and make provisions for it."

Lydia's expression darkens as she sets her teacup down. "There is no excuse for what's happening to the Amazon rainforest, the living climate stabiliser for the planet."

We turn our attention.

"Like what?" Layla asks.

"They're bulldozing sections of it," Lydia says quietly.

"Why? How can it be allowed?" I ask in shock.

"It's hard to believe, but it's to build runways and roads for a climate conference."

We fall silent. I catch my breath as my hopes tighten into a knot of disbelief.

"It's beyond ironic," she whispers.

"It's absurd," Layla adds.

"No," Pascal murmurs, eyes narrowing. "It's unforgiveable."

"Surely there should be a World Climate Forum to stop this kind of thing happening," Lydia says with passion. "One grounded in truth and trust, shaped by scientist, indigenous leaders and people who care."

"Where climate action," says Pascal, looking up from his nautical map, "is informed and considerate without getting lost in foggy statements and hollow promises."

Anil adjusts her cap. "Let's not get side tracked. I need to focus on the wish in hand. Please keep on reading, Liam."

Liam picks up one of the biscuits, dips it in his tea and

continues. "'We're solving problems with arid soil and helping it recover, but time is short – just five to ten years to act. Bunds are like smiles in the soil. Curved mounds, shaped to catch rain that would otherwise run away. They hold it just long enough for seeds to take root.'"

"Earth smiles," I say. "Every drop of rain, a gift. We forget how lucky we are to have so much of it."

Liam taps the magazine. "It always amazes me how simple actions, like digging a crescent of earth, can trigger such transformation."

"Amsterdam is not far from my kingdom," says Pascal. "You could head there to find out more about the regreening projects in Africa and meet us further south at Scheveningen harbour in The Hague, or whatever works best," he says, looking at his chart. "I'll happily sail you there. It's not far."

"What a wonderful invitation," says Anil.

"We leave for The Hague with the forest food growers on board on Tuesday," says Kobalos.

"Your dinner is on Monday, isn't it?" asks Pascal. "Why not join us in The Hague and I'll sail you to Amsterdam to learn about the bunds from there. You could meet us on the boat on Tuesday evening in time for supper?"

"Sounds perfect," I say, smiling. "And a chance to share our adventure in the Pixie Kingdom."

Pascal leans forwards. "Ah-ha. What's your mission

about, Sky?"

"I'm not one hundred per cent sure," I admit. "Don't laugh, but a duck named Salter keeps appearing in my dreams, warning me that there's no time to loose and that I must get myself out there without delay. It feels urgent."

"It's why we're leaving for the Pixie Kingdom after breakfast," says Anil. "We'll join The Lady co-hosting the dinner and plant a few dreams to pave the way."

Layla and I would rather work together, not on planting dreams, but keeping the Murmurers away from the guests and out of the house."

I nod in agreement.

"Murmurers drift in where people forget to care," Layla says. "They don't need fog. They create it in people's minds."

"It will be essential not to let doubt in," Kobalos remarks.

"We can't interfere with outcomes," I say. "But Lydia, Anil and I will plant the beginning of dreams that could develop into ideas on the evening."

"The dinner in your kingdom was your idea in the first place, Pascal," I smile.

"And it was Robbie who found the industrialist-turned-conservationist to plant the seed of the dream to host them," Anil adds.

"*Les Résolveur de Notre Temps*," sings Pascal humorously as Robbie, the robin, arrives right on cue, enthusiastically joining in the chorus at the top of his voice.

"Who will be there?" Kobalos asks with curiosity.

"People who can make a difference," Anil replies, sitting up straighter. "Or, as it's well described in Pascal's mother tongue – the solvers of our time or the weather, depending on who's translating. In this case, both," she winks.

I nod. "Anil and I will concentrate on The Lady, but according to my dream, we'll need to pay attention to a key player from the insurance world." I scan the guest list in my mind and share it with Lydia.

"Emmanuel," she says thoughtfully. "Let me try my hand with him. I'd like to learn more about the subject and how he might fit into the bigger picture."

"We can help you there," I say, looking at her. "Right, Anil?"

"The Winds of Change are taking us to an insurance office this afternoon to oversee a meeting between The Lady and, I expect, Emmanuel. Although they didn't mention his name, they shared quite a bit of information about him."

Anil suddenly jumps up mid-sentence and starts riffling through the maps on the shelf behind her. She quickly sketches a drawing on the back of a paper napkin and hands it to Lydia.

"These are the regions he is concerned about, particularly when it comes to insurance claims due to extreme weather."

"Claims?" Lydia says, confused. "Soil is my subject, and I don't even know the meaning of insurance, but Caroline, my friend in Kenya, is clued up on the subject. I'll ask for her help."

Anito presses his hands together with respect. "Businesses are all about hierarchies no different from our ecosystems, but with different names.

"Dreams planted in fertile minds should yield good results," Kobalos says thoughtfully. "Consider the notion I am learning from my agricultural studies: '*If you think you can do it alone, you are not thinking big enough.*'"

A sudden blast of wind rattles the sails tied to the mast.

"I hope there isn't a storm brewing," Pascal says, glancing at the clouds.

"Oh, no, not at all!" Anil pipes up. "It's the Winds of Change come to pick us up."

* * *

Without warning, the Winds of Change sweep us off our feet. One moment we're waving goodbye, the next, we're gliding on a warm, buoyant cushion of air, like a magic carpet riding through the sky. We waft over the North Sea, the harbour disappearing behind us, the others left on the boat, gape and scratch their heads, mouths half-open in astonishment. Robbie weaves patterns through the air, looping the loop, soaring and gliding, riding the tailwinds that push us forward with purpose.

"This is lovely," I say, watching the water ripple far below. "It reminds me of the West Wind, the way it saved us from the storm as a cloud shaped like a peregrine falcon."

Anil tunes in to the whispering language of the Winds. "They're sent by Queen Titania," she says, "not just to reach the Pixie Kingdom as fast as possible."

Anil's brow furrows as she listens intently. She gestures in the air, requesting a pencil and paper. "Thanks," she says, quickly scribbling down the facts. "It's more serious than that, I'm afraid. The Winds say hurricanes are forming, not in anger, but in protest. They say we need to step up and acknowledge their message, as they are preparing a demonstration to highlight the urgency of cooling the planet."

"Any specifics?" Lydia asks, her voice edged with unease.

Anil concentrates. "They say the Four Winds are planning a chain of storms - intense, deliberate, and devastating to rapidly intensify into hurricanes during the

Atlantic hurricane season. And that's not all. Dry air is building up over Los Angeles. Fires will follow. These events aren't accidents. They're desperate signals, climate warnings written in the wind and flaring in flames."

Layla's eyes widen. "Are we meant to stop them?"

"No one can stop them," Lydia murmurs, shaking her head. "Not yet." She stares towards the horizon. "The land is too dry. One spark, and everything could catch fire like kindling wood."

Layla hugs her elbows. "Planting trees helps, but what's the point if they're reduced to ash before they can provide shade?"

The silence that follows is thick with helplessness. But something stirs in my memory. My dream, and the duck named Salter painting clouds whiter with misty sea spray, bouncing the heat of the sun back into outer space. "There is a way," I say. "It would buy the planet some time for changes to be put in place. Moving to clean energy isn't an overnight process."

Anito leans forward, running his fingers gently over the surface of the cloud, as if stroking a frightened animal. "We can't just sit here," he says. "Hurricanes are faster now, stronger. They scream in from nowhere, rip through homes, drown towns, and leave people standing waist-high in water where their living rooms used to be."

"The Winds of Change don't want this," Anil says. "They're begging for help. The storms are a cry, not of rage, but exhaustion. They're overwhelmed. Pollution feeds their fury. They're not attacking. They're reacting."

"That's the whole point," says Anito. "And the only way to calm the storms is to stop feeding them with pollution. That means us."

"The power of the collective voice," I say. "Especially children."

Anito nods. "Exactly. Schoolchildren have the clarity adults have lost. They care more than anyone realises."

Anil pulls a piece of paper from her pocket.

"Look at my notes on this map," she says, handing it to Lydia. "They're a bit rough, but read with my jottings on the back of that paper napkin, it should make some sense."

Lydia frowns, turning the sketch sideways and retrieving the paper napkin. "I don't get it," she mumbles. But something shifts. Her eyes sharpen and she catches her breath.

"It's not just a warning. It's an opportunity," Lydia whispers, clutching the paper napkin as if it were treasure. For a moment, there is silence, but then her eyes light up. "I've got it!" she exclaims in sudden amazement.

Lydia does not allow us to enter further into her thoughts, but the glint in her eye indicates that something remarkable is developing. She gives Anil a nod of recognition. Something has begun.

* * *

As we ride the breeze towards the Pixie Kingdom, hair streaming behind us and cheeks flushed with excitement, I receive a message from Sol to listen in on Max and Valentine's progress. I turn to Lydia and motion for her to join me. We instantly tune in, eavesdropping on a windswept field in Northumberland, where Max and Valentine are walking alongside Mark, the farm manager.

"I had no idea growing healthy, nutritious fruit and vegetables would be so unprofitable," Valentine says, raising an eyebrow at Mark. "Where's the incentive?"

Mark scratches his chin. "You're not wrong. Folk've got used to cheap food – and who can blame 'em? Wages haven't kept up."

Max nods solemnly. "It's a vicious circle. The pressure to keep prices low pushes farmers to overproduce. We end up striping the soil of its nutrients, with no chance to rest or regenerate. It's like flogging a tired horse."

Mark lowers his gaze. "That was me, alright, for years," he admits. "Always one eye on yield, the other on profit. Too afraid to be the first to try something new - s'pose I doubted myself," he chuckles, tapping the brim of his cap. "But then… I started dreaming. Not just any dreams. Sounds daft, but they were dreams about *soil.* About the goodness beneath our feet, if only we'd treat it right."

He looks up. "I saw it, plain as day. When the land's

alive, the crops are stronger, more resistant, and more nourishing. The dream took root. And no one's been able to sway me since," he adds, with a wry grin.

"The power of belief," Valentine murmurs. "That's what drew Max to Klim, isn't it?"

"Absolutely," Max replies. "They understood what we are trying to build. Gave us solid advice when we were at a crossroads."

"Yah," Mark mutters, kicking a stone with the toe of his boot. "Stranded by the government's so-called 'sustainable farming incentive'."

Max puffs out his cheeks, leaning back on his heals. "It was great, but by the time my application went through, they paused the scheme. Too many farmers, too little money."

Mark frowns. "But how then will you manage? How will you grow good, healthy food people can actually afford, without help to cover the costs?"

Valentine takes Max's arm and gives it a squeeze. "By believing and living with hope."

Max smiles back at her. "And by trusting the land," he says.

Mark tilts his head. "How's that work?"

"Sustainable farming *does* pay off. Rich soil holds water better. Crops survive drought and floods. We cut back on manmade fertilisers, which saves money in the long run."

Mark gives a low whistle. "Since signing up with Klim, we've got allies. I've learnt how to grow crops that stand their ground, even in wild weather. A system that gives more than it takes." He punches the air with pride. "We're the living proof, then."

Max smiles, but his eyes remain thoughtful. "Still, we're up against supermarket prices. That's the hard part. But I'm starting to believe in wishes again." He pauses. "Hidden hands inside the tangle of red tape, people who care are trying to fix things."

"Quiet heroes," says Valentine, catching his meaning. "Working behind the scenes, pushing ideas like seeds in soil."

"And doing it with courage," Max answers. "Little by little, shifting the tide."

"We're nearly there," Anil interrupts.

Lydia and I cast one last look at the fields and send an emoji to thank Sol.

As the Winds of Change carry us southward, the Northumberland scene lingers like the faint scent of something freshly planted, just beneath the surface, waiting to bloom. The first green shoots of a better future are breaking through, fragile, but fearless. Brave enough to take root, rise up, lift their faces to the sky, and grow.

10

A SMOKE SCREEN

Welcomed by Arianne into her home in the enchanted forest, we settle into a treehouse she has kindly reserved for us to share. Just next door, Robbie takes a nap in a cosy bird box, exhausted after the journey.

"I'm so pleased you're early," Arianne exclaims, clapping her hands. "And arriving on a magic carpet, no less! Very rizz," she beams, leading us to a shaded balcony overlooking the forest. "I've got some simple home-grown food in the larder," she says with effortless generosity, laying out a hearty lunch of forest food and freshly gathered herbs.

"You'll want to rest this afternoon before planting any dreams, that's for sure!" she adds with a knowing smile, handing us each a plate of pixie pâté. "Have you thought about what they'll be?"

"We're working on it," I reply with a playful wink. "But first, we're off to meet a man named Emmanuel – he might just help us shape those dreams into something real."

* * *

In a sleek, glass-walled office high above the city, Emmanuel, a confident, competent executive, sits behind a polished desk, framed by clouds and the skyline. At a knock at the door, he stands. The Lady enters, composed, a parcel tucked under her arm.

A soft whoosh of smoke slithers beneath the door behind her, curling upwards like a living thing, invisible to Emmanuel but not to us. The air thickens, heavy with the stench of scorched wires and sulphur. Acrid. Anil and I keep our distance. We had doused ourselves in rosewater before leaving, but its protective sweetness is already losing strength and fading.

The smoke doesn't drift away; instead, it clings to Emmanuel like a shadow, poisoning his thoughts and nudging decisions off course. It coils near the air vents, moving with purpose rather than simply drifting. Its intentions are relentless: to stall, to confuse, and to stifle any prospects for change.

Anil and I hover beside The Lady's ears, shielding her from their murmured doubts. She unwraps the parcel with care, pulling out a model boat made of balsa wood, painted in red and white, and places it on Emmanuel's desk.

"Beautiful, isn't it?" she says.

Emmanuel picks up the boat, eyebrows raised. "Intriguing," he says slowly. "Do tell me more." A flicker of suspicion enters his mind. *What's this woman trying to pull?* He looks at his watch. *I'll give her fifteen minutes. No more.*

"It's a spray boat that could help cool the planet," The Lady replies, peering over tortoiseshell glasses. "Designed by Professor Stephen Salter for Marine Cloud ReBrightening."

Emmanuel frowns. The boat has no sails. *Is this a joke?*

"No sails?" he asks. "How can they move?"

The Lady leans forward, a twinkle in her eye. "They're powered by the wind, but not in the usual way. These boats are guided remotely using flettner rotors - tall spinning cylinders that harness the wind's energy far more efficiently than traditional sails. No fuel. Zero emissions," The Lady says. "As they glide over the ocean, they spray fine droplets of seawater into the sky, brightening clouds. Brighter clouds reflect more sunlight away from the earth, acting like a giant sunhat to keep the planet cool, if you like."

Emmanuel looks sceptical. "I see. But not without risk."

The Lady nods. "That's where you come in. You understand risk better than most. What we're talking about is collaboration between nature and human ingenuity – designed not to disrupt, but to protect. These boats could help prevent irreversible tipping points. And if we don't act soon, the insurance industry may be overwhelmed by claims no policy can cover."

Behind him, the smoke thickens. No longer is there just one invisible Murmurer, but many. These aren't the cloaked figures that shadow people as they go, whispering into ears on street corners. These ones inhabit the cracks in the system, nourished by fear. They are shades of grey, with no place to hide among rainbow sprites. They slip through ducts and drift like mist, stifling creativity and choking resolve.

We brace ourselves. Our rosewater has all but worn off. Emmanuel taps his chin. He jots down a rough calculation on the back of an envelope.

'*Why you?*' murmurs a voice. '*You're no scientist. Don't be reckless. Don't stand out.*' Emmanuel's fingers tighten around the pencil.

"Why me," he asks aloud.

The Lady's reply is steady. "Because insurers like you are already paying the price of climate disasters. And if we wait, they'll come a day when the losses are simply uninsurable. But if the industry helps fund solutions – real solutions – you won't just reduce risk. You'll take the lead."

Emmanuel exhales, eyes scanning the sealed windows, unsure whether the air-conditioning is working.

"You're saying we should help invest in this as a long-term strategy? Fewer disasters, fewer claims… and a more stable world?"

"Exactly," The Lady smiles. "It's not just business. It's survival. Food security. Homes. Hope. Step up now, and others will follow."

Emmanuel folds his arms, guarded. "I'd need solid

proof this wouldn't cause new weather problems. Could your team of scientists provide that?"

The Lady doesn't blink. "They'll have to."

He raises an eyebrow, tapping his desk rhythmically. "There's opposition," he says, standing. "I don't want to be the first." He extends his hand to shake. "But you're right. We can't keep paying out on disasters on this scale. Something has to change."

"Maybe it's time," she says, taking his hand, "to stop reacting to catastrophe, and start preventing it."

Anil and I linger beside Emmanuel, tuning into the hum of his thoughts. His mind is in overdrive, bustling with conflict, calculations, ambitions swamped with doubts.

'I could form a consortium… share the risk… but what if it fails? What if I look foolish?'

The Murmurers press in, whispering: *'Not your job. Let someone else take the fall.'*

Anil and I exchange a glance. The smoke is in every crevice of the building, living in the pipework, coiled in the shadows.

The Lady picks up her package and turns to leave, but in the corners of the room, she senses something faint - grey shadows that resemble wisps of smoke. They are barely visible, silent, and watchful, exuding a low hum of unease. Their presence isn't loud, but it weighs heavy in the air, thick with negative energy. The Lady pauses and then smiles gently, feeling the warmth of our colour glow rise like a protective shield around her.

"Thank you for seeing me," she says. "There's something wrong with the system, you know. Too much grey and not enough colour to brighten things up."

The shadows still. Unsettled, as The Lady closes the door behind her.

I send word to Lydia. Tonight, she'll need to weave a carefully crafted dream for Emmanuel - one sewn with hope, stitched with courage, and threaded with possibility - a dream able to take root to grow as his own.

"At least he'll be at away from his office for the weekend," Anil says, already bounding down the stairwell, eager to be out in the open air.

Outside, we find a tree and settle beneath its branches.

"The dream I'll shape for The Lady," I say, "will be of winds that carry promises, ice at the poles gleaming like silver mirrors, catching the sun and deflecting it back - a planet cooling in careful hands. If Lydia does well with Emmanuel," I whisper, "he'll be a beacon - a tide of change to support her, steady and unstoppable."

"What about the children?" Anil reminds me softly. "Can I do one too? I'd like to pass on the dream of Queen Titania standing with her wand lowered in a far away land. Her words turned to mist, and from the cracked soil, green shoots emerged."

"Done," I nod. "You plant yours tonight. I'll plant mine tomorrow."

"Deal," she grins. "And I'll show the role of children enriching the soils of Africa. The Lady will feel it and take it from there."

* * *

Arriving in the square where the changemaker lives, Anil and I find Layla and Anito sitting watchfully on top of a sentry box next to his home.

"Any sign of the Murmurers?" we ask.

"Only the invisible kind," Anito replies. "When we arrived, they swirled like smoke trapped in the rafters – smoggy, foggy, like Murmurers whispering in the draft. They've thinned now, but something tells me they're not entirely gone," he says. "We're also keeping an eye out for the Mistress of Missed Momentum. We had a whiff she might make an appearance tonight, didn't we, Layla?"

"Yes. They say she turns up as a single sigh in a boardroom, a forgotten agenda item, or a paragraph redrafted to say 'not yet'. Watch the corners of the room for her. She rarely shows herself, but her fingerprints are always on the record. She walks beside boardroom chairs and conference tables, whispering 'further study', 'more reports', 'not our jurisdiction', 'be cautious', 'not *your* head on the block'," says Layla, holding up a spray bottle. "The invisible ones hate the smell of anything nice, especially rosewater."

"And we've found that fairy dust also makes the unseen ones disappear," Anito adds, holding up a multi-coloured sprinkle box. "We have no defence against the cloaked figures who walk the corridors of power like faceless lobbyists, murmuring doubt into the ears of decision-makers. They don't flee from rosewater; instead, they simply vanish into the shadows and wait."

We cross our fingers and wish Layla and Anito good luck just as a taxi pulls up. Out steps The Lady. She rings the doorbell of the house with a flag flying above its mantle. We follow her through an extremely high entrance door into a marble-clad hallway.

"What a welcoming smell of… rosewater," she suggests, sniffing the air, greeted by a young woman wearing an apron. "Would it be alright to have a sneak preview of our dinner with Ali in the Kitchen?" The Lady asks.

"*Mais oui*," she says with a curtsy. "I'm getting everything ready for you upstairs. The house owner will not be here until later. He said to start without him."

"Thank you, we appreciate your hard work in making everything look so nice," says The Lady, admiring a vase of flowers on the hall table.

"A terrible smell of smoke came through an open window and filled the house. It was acrid and strange – it clung to the curtains. I fumigated the house, but…"

Anil and I exchange a glance. "Anito was right. They were here."

The Lady smiles, "all I can smell is rosewater, and the fragrant flowers."

We breathe sighs of relief and follow The Lady into a gleaming kitchen where preparation is under way.

"Wow! How delicious," we say to each other, gaping as Ali opens the fridge…

11

WHEN THE TRUTH BE TOLD

The meeting room was warm with quiet anticipation, a sense of underlying tension simmering beneath polite conversation and the clink of teaspoons. The Lady welcomes guests on the first floor and pours out tea and coffee with practiced ease, pausing for light remarks and ripples of gentle laughter. To an observer, it might have appeared to be just another civilised gathering, with nothing out of the ordinary. However, as Anil and I hover above The Lady, we sense her breath tighten slightly, filled with an undercurrent of apprehension – a storm of words she hopes to deliver without losing her train of thought. We settle on her shoulders, offering quiet encouragement while everyone takes their place around the table. Lydia stays close to Emmanuel.

Jacob, a filmmaker in a white shirt and straight tie, watches The Lady closely, storyboarding ideas in his mind that translate truth into light and movement, evoking an understanding that quickens the heart. Across from him, a woman with long dark hair and gentle eyes reflects on former colleagues, alumni of an oil giant. She wonders, not for the first time, whether they might be willing to invest in repairing the damage they once helped create.

Robert, an impact investor, sits near the head of the table, his pen tapping lightly. His mind is sharp with strategy, yet he listens with his heart.

Some guests lean back, unreadable. Others fold their arms, restless. Anil and I listen to their unspoken hopes, the creeping doubts, and quiet readiness, some wondering why they are here.

The Lady smooths the skirt of her dress, standing before the seated group.

"Ladies and gentlemen," she begins. The curtains billow, and I notice someone in a dark cloak slip into the shadows at the back of the room.

"Welcome to this roundtable meeting, which I am pleased to co-host with the house owner. He will join us shortly. With many remarkably influential people gathered here, I almost lost my nerve to say what I must. Yet I believe, quite stubbornly, in freedom of speech - And, perhaps more importantly, in truth. However uncomfortable, truth is the only lens through which we might hope to see problems clearly enough to solve them."

She pauses, letting the silence sit. "You see," she continues, "I once believed that the greatest environmental threats were biodiversity loss, ecosystem collapse and climate change. I thought that, armed with thirty years of good science, we could fix them. But I was wrong. The real problems are extraction, selfishness, hypocrisy, greed, and stagnation. And for those, my friends, we do not need more science. We need a transformation of heart. Of how we speak, and listen, communicate and act. Alas, lawyers and scientists, brilliant as they may be, lack the skill of being heard by an audience beyond academia."

A ripple of uneasy laughter runs around the table.

"I shall tell you a story," she says, her eyes twinkling. "It is not a fairy tale – although I dearly wish it were. It's a story about the air we breathe, the water we drink and the world our children will inherit."

The room grows taut with silence.

"Once upon a time, the Earth lived in balance. Oceans breathed in and out. Winds whispered rather than howled. Ice gleamed at the poles like silver mirrors, reflecting sunlight to keep us cool. And bright marine clouds did the same and cooled the oceans and the planet. But something changed. *We* changed - we burned; we polluted; we consumed and guzzled without a second thought. And so, the Earth began to overheat, and nature, patient no more, reacted. The ice melted, the seas rose, the clouds diminished, and the oceans warmed. The winds hollered in protest. And yet, we sat at dinner tables, not unlike the one we shall enjoy tonight, nibbling and quibbling, as though debate could soothe a storm… Waiting - always waiting, for someone else to act.

"But here's the rub: time does not wait for committees. The atmosphere does not pause for feasibility studies. The ice does not consult a minister before it melts. While papers are shuffled and speeches are polished, the tipping points TIP." She turns, fixing her eyes first on Emmanuel, moving around the table, anchoring each listener with her stare. "Floods do not call a meeting before they wash away homes. Droughts do not wait politely for policy revisions before they turn fields to dust.

"And the children? Believe you me, they are watching. They will repeat the words of Greta Thunberg and ask: *'what did you do while the world burned?'*"

The door swings open and the house owner enters quietly and sits beside her. The Lady gives him a nod of welcome and a warm smile before continuing, her voice gaining in force.

"The answer isn't in more promises or ponderous discussions. It is about action, real, tangible action. Now," she says, leaning forward. "Professor Stephen Salter offered us a breathing space through Marine Cloud ReBrightening, misting the air with seawater to shield the planet from scorching heat. But instead of embracing his inventions, we left it gathering dust, not because it wouldn't work, but because no one with enough knowledge, power or money had the courage to act.

"So let me be plain. This is not about the distant future. This is about the here and now. About whether you, sitting here tonight, have the integrity to act beyond your own interests and invest in survival itself."

She lifts her chin. "Professor Sir David King has given you the science, the facts, the brutal truth. The cost of delay is no longer a number. It is a *reckoning*." She softens her tone, yet speaks through clenched teeth, wearing a frown. "The money is here in this room, along with the power. The only missing ingredient is the will."

The Lady rises to her full height, exuding grace infused with quiet fury. "Fund the research. Fund hope. Fund the future that is the birthright of humanity. Together, with courage in our hearts and our heads held high, we can rewrite this story. Not as a fairy tale, but as a reflection of the real world. The choice is yours. History will not be kind to those who hesitated when the answers were still within reach and there was a chance to rebrighten our world again."

With that, The Lady takes her seat, and a hush falls over the room, not from fear or confusion, but from the weight of something undeniable: a quiet, passionate determination, stilling their restless minds.

Taking his cue, Emmanuel slowly rises to his feet. He nods respectfully towards the house owner.

"I represent a global insurer," he says, looking at nobody in particular. "Our entire model is built on anticipating risk, but we can no longer keep up. Climate change is accelerating faster than our calculations allow. If we don't act now, even the most comprehensive insurance policy won't protect us from what's coming. When I accepted the invitation to dinner tonight, I had my reservations. I thought I might simply observe, reflect, and remain silent. However, I had a dream last night and another the night before. The first was a nightmare of catastrophe: I saw Los Angeles blackened by fire and Florida torn apart by storm. The second showed a solution, a way forward."

He looks to The Lady and nods. "You spoke of time and the cost of inaction. I agree. The evidence is clear, and so is the science. At my insurance company, we don't just insure against loss; we help societies manage risk. Now, we must manage that risk on a global scale.

"If insurers wait for disasters to strike, they will always be a step behind. But what if we could literally insure the atmosphere by investing in measures to prevent disasters from occurring in the first place?" he says casually. "For example, we could use Marine Cloud ReBrightening to cool the air and help prevent temperatures from rising, bringing them down instead. The cost of one summer's payout in California could fund the research and implementation needed to buy us breathing space that keeps millions of people safe." Emmanuel takes a breath. "As I've mentioned, I hadn't planned to speak tonight; I thought I would just listen. But sometimes a speech moves you so deeply that remaining silent feels like a betrayal. The Lady emphasised truth and urgency. We don't need more committees; we need courage."

He glances at The Lady and around the table. "As someone in risk management, I'm not easily shaken. This isn't just climate risk anymore; it's a risk to our very existence. We must adapt our thinking accordingly, flip the model, and instead of paying out after a catastrophe, we need to prevent it from happening in the first place. This means funding projects like Marine Cloud ReBrightening, which will cool the planet responsibly. It should not be treated as a side bet, last resort, experiment, or afterthought, but rather as a frontline intervention as our defence - a global insurance policy for Earth itself."

Emmanuel's voice sharpens, ringing clear: "If we succeed, we will gain time to transition to green energy. If we wait, we will burn."

A murmur of approval grows around the table.

"I've already initiated the process. We're exploring joining the World Climate Forum and establishing a Climate Resilience Fund. A portion of that fund will go directly to Marine Cloud ReBrightening research and implementation, giving us more time while we decarbonise and transition." He smiles, grim but sure. "It's a small step, but a significant one. The only thing worse than inaction… is regret."

Emmanuel sits down, and the reaction that follows is not of hesitation, but one of momentum, humming through the room and striking chords. Guests rise to clap and cheer for him, with The Lady leading the applause, her claps loud and certain - a great sense of relief fills the air. Anil and I join in, but our homage is toward Lydia, who bows to Anil and returns the compliment.

"Your map of destruction, dictated by the Winds of Change, along with Emmanuel's area of expertise that you outlined on the back of the paper napkin – that's what made the difference," she says, allowing herself the smallest of smiles.

I turn to congratulate Anil, and as I gently tap her on the back, I notice her violet glow growing stronger, deepening into a rich purple.

The Lady slips away for a quiet moment to check that all is well in the kitchen, where faint aromas of rosemary, citrus, and melting butter are wafting up to the first floor. Anil and I follow her into the dining room, astonished by the scene before us. The table is adorned with silver candelabras with flames dancing rhythmically in the evening light. Hand-painted porcelain plates, bearing the house owner's coat of arms, are set at each place setting.

The Lady refers to her table plan, which took days to finalise, and carefully places handwritten name cards above each plate. She steps back and takes a deep, steady breath. Her speech had gone well. Emmanuel had come through. Although The Lady appears tired, she also seems taller, as if she had finally mustered the courage to speak her truth and been truly heard.

"Where had the words come from?" she asks herself, shaking her head. "Something out there is helping me find my voice," she thinks, her eyes widening. For the first time that evening, she allows herself a private smile - and so do I.

12

A CHANGE OF HEART

As guests begin to mingle, a low murmur stirs at the back of the meeting room – subtle, like a ripple beneath the surface. Most take no notice, absorbed in conversation and distracted by the clink of glasses. But I notice, immediately. Eyes sharp, I catch sight of a figure slipping quietly away, not toward the main staircase like the others, but through the door to an anteroom, moving with deliberate haste, trying to escape without notice.

"Look, Anil, a Murmurer," I whisper, clutching her by the arm.

Anil turns just in time to catch a glimpse of a dark cloak disappearing around the landing, sneaking down the stairs to the front hall. "Spying on us," she says. "He must have slipped in when we were too busy listening. Something tells me the Queen of Hearts sent him to report back to her. But I'm no longer afraid of her. Are you?"

"No," I say, somewhat surprised to find that I felt that way. "It was The Lady's speech, so aligned with Queen Titania's values. I just hope the Murmurer won't twist her words."

"Murmurers have to digest the truth before they can turn it upside down," Anil says. "When he reports it, it's sure to be the full transcript. Come on, let's track him down and figure out what's going on."

I quickly message Anito: *Hold the fort with Layla. Lydia will stay in the house. A Murmurer managed to sneak in. We think the Queen of Hearts may have sent him as an envoy. Off to find out.*

Anil and I slip through the sash window into a night thick with shadows. A figure scurries across the square – the Murmurer, hunched and quick on his feet. We follow him as he vanishes beneath the portico of the local theatre, pulls out his phone, and makes a call to Wonderland.

We tune into The Queen of Hearts, fast asleep. When the phone rings, she opens her eyes. It's not just the sound of the phone that awakens her, but a strange current of energy that jolts her bolt upright in bed. She listens intently, not interrupting until he finishes.

Lying low on the flat roof, we hear his voice drift up through the darkness, muffled yet urgent, reciting The Lady's speech almost word for word.

"No kidding," I whisper. "At least he's accurate."

"It was sumptuous, the setting. I mean… privileged," ventures the voice.

"Privileged?" the Queen repeats sharply. "Oh, spare me the sighs! Nobody chooses what cradle they are born into! It's what you do with the cards you're dealt! That's the game." She flings her arms wide as if addressing him in person. "Authenticity – that's the goal! Whether it's an Inuit welcoming you into his igloo or a Lakota sharing their tepee – it's how you hold the door open that counts, not the size of the house!" she shouts into the mouthpiece, warming to her theme. "Don't you dare twist it into guilt, or we'll lose the very people we need! Wealth marching at our side, not running for the hills! Now – repeat what The Lady said about the material world."

"Selfishness, hypocrisy, greed and stagnation," the Murmurer mumbles.

"My words! Those were *my* words!" she exclaims, clapping her hands with glee. "Go on! Tell me again about the lawyers and the scientists!"

"The Lady said the world needs a magical transformation, but that lawyers and scientists often struggle to speak plainly enough for people to follow."

"Hah! No surprise there!" The Queen of Hearts throws back her covers and swings her legs out of bed. "I'm a Queen, and I know how to speak so the people listen! And what of courage?" she prompts, raising an eyebrow.

"The Lady said 'Together, with courage in our hearts and our heads held high, we can rewrite this story. Not as a fairy tale, but one rooted in the material world.'"

The Queen of Hearts gasps with joy. "Stop your murmurings! Change the story!" she orders. Her voice resonates around the chamber, growing bolder with every word. "At last! Not just Titania's fairy tales, but real deeds in the real world! Finally, someone out there understands that we don't live in a bedtime story, but can take action to awaken people and make our voices heard."

For a moment, we sit there, speechless, as if the whole world has tilted a tiny bit closer in our favour.

I turn to Anil, astonished. "She's stepping boldly into the real world, with the power of fire firmly under her control."

"She's unpredictable," Anil replies. "I just hope she remembers how she feels now in the morning and that the fire hasn't gone out."

"Good thinking. I'll warn Queen Titania in case she has another change of heart."

* * *

Queen Titania had risen early unsettled by my message from the Pixie Kingdom: *The Queen of Hearts is blazing into the real world. The fire is alive. Now is the moment to reach her! - With reverence, Sky.*

Titania did not take warnings lightly. In truth, she rarely accepted advice. But this situation was different. She had tuned into our evening, watched it unfold live, and noticed a slight shift – in the wind, in the atmosphere, and now, evidently, in the one royal figure most likely to bark *'Off with your head!'* at the slightest moonblink of provocation.

Titania waited at the edge of the ornamental garden, where the dew sparkled like diamonds under the early morning sun. Suddenly, the palace doors few open, and out marched the Queen of Hearts – a striking figure in crimson slippers and a wildly patterned dressing gown, her hair in disarray beneath a lopsided crown. With a theatrical thud, she slammed the door shut behind her.

"There you are," she booms.

"Good morning, my dear," Titania smiles.

"Don't *my dear* me," the Queen huffs. "I'm still recovering from the shock of realisation!" she declares, striding across the grass like a general on a mission. "The Lady ignited a flame that even the Murmurers couldn't snuff out."

"No country can stop the winds, nor contain the seas," says Titania, "but there's magic in cooperation. Now that clarity has struck, what do you propose?"

"A position," declares the Queen of Hearts, planting her hands firmly on her hips. "*Officer in Chief of Global Unity and Renewal.* And let us not forget," she declares, raising her voice, "the hideous toll of warfare – not only on lives, but on lands, skies, and seas. Bombs poison rivers, tanks scar the earth, and smoke chokes the air. If I am to lead, I will speak as fiercely for peace as I once did for power."

"I agree," Queen Titania says calmly, "but shouting isn't a strategy. As an Officer of Global Unity and Renewal, you'll need more than outrage – you'll need influence. Guilt fades quickly; agreement endures. Awakening humanity requires not just volume, but vision."

"My voice rouses people. They hear me!" the Queen of Hearts insists, her eyes ablaze.

"That's true," Titania replies gently, "but mine stills rooms, and calms kings and councils into listening."

The Queen of Hearts straightens up with unwavering determination. "I propose a pact!" she announces, flinging her arms above her head. "You rally the children, and I'll set off some firecrackers to stir the grown-ups who claim to lead but do little more than sit and wait!"

Titania's lips reveal a hint of a smile. "A pact… not for power, but for purpose."

"Exactly," the Queen of Hearts nods. "Nature needs a seat at the table of human systems, not just in spirit, but in structure. Forests and rivers should be granted legal rights, with judges upholding them in court. I'll call for reformers to rewrite the rules, placing the natural world at the heart of economic political decisions. If the world is on fire, I'll fight fire with fire, and rewrite the law books to do it. We will stop the Murmurers from spreading doubt and distraction, and start *working*. Your fairy tales can wake the dreamers. But I've got the voice to wake the sleepwalkers with something stronger than bedtime stories – a proper wake-up call."

And so the pact was struck. The Queen of Hearts plops down onto a stone bench and heaves a sigh of relief.

"I've spent too long barking at shadows while you sang to the moon. But The Lady has ignited something within me that I don't want to lose again."

Titania sits beside her. "Let's not let that spark fade, shall we? There is a world to heal, and children are already leading the way."

The Queen of Hearts nods. "I'll bring the drama… and follow your direction."

They sit together in a comfortable silence, watching the early sun stretch across the garden, two queens, not ruling, but ready to serve.

Above them, the morning wind rises, brisk, scented with sea salt. Somewhere far off, gulls cry over open water and a distant bell chimes the hour.

The Queen of Hearts reaches into the folds of her nightgown and draws out a deck of cards, worn at the edges. "No more hiding behind tricks," she says. "Let's deal a new hand."

Titania smiles as they rise together, walking side by side through the dew-drenched garden. The first gusts of the Winds of Change stir the leaves into motion – soft at first, but gathering strength. Their mood shifts, transformed not just by the words but also by the intention behind them.

They seek not power, but purpose, carrying the spark where it is needed most – in the hearts of those ready to take action.

* * *

"About time!" Liam shouts from the stern, tossing a spoon in the air and catching it with the flair of a street performer.

"We were starting to think you'd stayed behind with The Lady for good!" he grins. "Our food forest friends are about to disembark."

We duck under a swinging lantern and step aboard.

"Oh dear," says Layla, eyeing a canvas bag brimming with asparagus and artichokes in a jute open weave sack from their farm. "Never mind - you can fill us in,"

The food forest farmers look up, sensing our arrival.

"I can smell elderflower… mixed with rosewater," says Sasha, rising to his feet. "Sorry to be leaving early after such a kind journey home."

"Yes, and a lovely supper too," adds Katja warmly.

"But farming waits for no one," Simon says, clasping Pascal's hand in farewell.

"And," Wytze adds with a grin, "if you want to make it to Amsterdam in time for breakfast, you'd better get a move on!"

Pascal gives a mock salute as the farmers step ashore. The boat rocks gently beneath us, timbers creaking against the stain of the ropes. Raising the anchor, we cut through the silky water, waving to the food forest farmers on the dock.

"Thanks for the veggies, nuts and delicious fruits," Kobalos calls across the darkening quay.

"They'll be freshly picked next time!" Sasha shouts, cupping his hands to carry his voice as we leave The Hague behind us.

Dropping our bags onto our hammocks we hurry back to the deck.

"Welcome," says Kobalos, turning with a warm smile. "Come, sit down beside me and tell us about your adventure in the Pixie Kingdom,"

We all start talking at once, our stories tumbling out, unfolding in turns, threading together like a tapestry, rich with colour, texture, and light, along with just as much laughter.

"It sounds fantastic," Pascal says with a sense of pride.

Liam perches on a crate, his legs dangling. "So let me get this straight," he says, wonder in his voice. "You, Anil, and Lydia floated above the guests, listening to every word?"

"Absolutely," I nod. "And from the way guests responded to the speeches, positive change is on its way."

Anito and Layla recount their story about how they dispelled the Murmurers before we arrived. Anil, filled with enthusiasm, acts out the scene in which we chase the hooded Murmurer who was spying for the Queen of Hearts.

Liam exhales slowly. "Ah, now I understand. That explains why she summoned for me."

"Flickeringfoxes! The Queen of Hearts summoned you?" I repeat with surprise.

Liam nods. "Instructing me to deliver her message in stories," he says. "She was very clear. She wants humanity to take action - not commanding them, but by standing beside young people, helping their hopes take root.

"She confided in me, too," Liam smiles with quiet satisfaction, "about her wake-up call that night, sitting up in bed to truly listen. Told me that for the first time, she didn't interrupt, but began to listen and understand. No shouting, no quick retorts. Just silence… and in that stillness, she said the truth dawned upon her. Not the kind that flatters or wins applause, but the kind of truth that stings. That sticks."

He pauses, looking out over the ocean, the lights of Amsterdam beginning to glimmer in the distance "She said she didn't feel ridiculed anymore, but included. Like she belonged as part of the story again."

Kobalos catches the wind in his sails as the skyline of Amsterdam sharpens, old buildings with gabled rooftops silhouetted against the stars, Central Station glowing on the riverbank.

"And if there's one thing I've learned in all my wanderings," Liam says, gently adjusting the sheets to steady our course, "it's that no one is ever just one person. Especially not the Queen of Hearts. The same fire that can destroy a forest can also light the way. Rage, when guided by purpose, becomes a powerful force. And now, she wields that power - not for revenge, nor for conquest, but as a quest for justice."

"So," says Lydia, biting into a succulent fig, "here we are in Amsterdam to meet Dennis Karpes and Peter Westerveld, the founders of *Justdiggit* in the morning. Afterwards, Sky and Anil will head to Kenya!"

Everyone gasps. I lean against the railing, drawing my knees to my chest, watching the water shimmer beneath the starlight. "It's perfect timing to meet them first and find out where we need to go," I say wistfully. "We'd like you to pave the way."

"I can only imagine what bunds look like," Anil murmurs softly. "Now I'll get to see them with my own eyes."

"Kenya is my second home," Lydia sighs with a faraway look in her eyes. "I'll set you up to meet my friend Caroline – she'll show you around."

Kobalos leans back, his green-tinged complexion catching the moonlight. "So, you're off to Kenya," he says, his eyes twinkling with interest. "The land holds deep memories. If you listen carefully, you might discover what it has to teach. A whisper of your next chapter awaits, ready to be discovered in the red soils and wide skies of Kenya."

He taps the deck gently with his toes. "Before humans stood upright and named the stars, they were part of the forest floor – threads in the great web of life, not separate from it. It's important to remember that before the bones and the brains and the buildings… there was mycelium. Silent. Clever. Connected. An underground network trading minerals and water with plants in exchange of sugars through photosynthesis." He pauses. "From those ancient swaps beneath the soil – minerals for sugars, life for life - grew the intricate ecosystems we know today. But somewhere along the way, humans forgot they were part of that mutual exchange."

The breeze twirls around us, playful, cool and mischievous. It lifts the scent of salt and twists my hair into wild, tight ringlets. Anil sits cross-legged beside me, her cap pulled low, eyes lost in the dark inky velvet water, watching starlight flicker across the surface, dancing in broken patterns, shimmering with mystery in the moonlight.

Pascal claps his hands. "All hands on deck! Liam – that rope, quick, before we drift and crash into the quay."

Liam springs ashore, nimble and alert, looping the ropes around the mooring bollards with practiced ease.

Pascal turns to me, his eyes glancing at the tall, narrow houses lining the water. "So tell me," he says. "Why Africa? Why now, even before meeting the Justdiggit team?"

I glance at Anil.

"It started with a dream," I say. "A dream of the

Nature Summit where we all met - sent to The Lady by Queen Titania herself. Anil planted another one that showed cracked earth turning green."

"The Winds of Change carried those dreams," Anil adds gently, "and turned them into stories at bedtime. Real stories that make you see what's possible."

"That's why they're taking us to Kenya," I say, excited, "to witness what happens when people stop waiting for help and start making something of what they have – proving that even from parched ground, something remarkable can grow."

13

SCHOOLS AT WORK

"Flickeringfoxes," I say as the Winds of Change deposit us on an acacia tree at a place where farmers are digging bunds.

"We've travelled all the way to Kenya in the blink of an eye while we were sleeping!" adds Anil, waking up in astonishment.

We breathe in the sweet air so different from anything we have known. It carries a scent so tender it feels like a welcome. Sweet and warm, it wraps around us like a sun-drenched shawl, part wild honey, part wood smoke, with hints of ripe mangoes falling softly to the earth. Beneath it all, there's a grounding smell of fertile soil kissed by recent rain, mingling with the faint floral aroma of frangipani in full bloom and wild hibiscus. It is the perfume of a land alive with promise: golden, generous, and vibrant.

Anil flies down and hovers just above the soil to examine it, her iridescent wings flutter in the light of the golden afternoon. Beneath her, the earth is soft and rich with life – but during our visit to Amsterdam, we learnt from Dennis and Peter just how fragile this delicate balance could so easily tip into ruin. Anil sighs in awe at the sight of the bunds. She presses her fingers into the dirt, feeling for its stories.

"Hello," calls a voice from high up in the tree. We look up to find a bright-eyed sprite with shiny blond hair lying on a banana leaf, smiling down at us, holding up a basket of exotic fruits.

"Hi, Caroline!" I wave.

"Lydia said you'd find us here," says Anil, brushing off bits of soil from her hands.

Caroline stretches. "I was snoozing, waiting for you to arrive," she says, as I fly up to join her. "The soil beneath your feet, Anil," she calls down, "has come back to life, thanks to the people who live here, and to caring companies like Justdiggit. They've helped farmers plant trees, dig water-saving bunds, and grow food again."

Caroline hands me a slice of mango. "And when a big storm ruins things," she adds, "a little help comes from Humanity-Insured so farmers can start over instead of giving up having lost their livelihood."

"Lydia told us you know loads about insurance," I say, biting into the succulent fruit.

Caroline nods. "It's my thing. Insurance can't stop a storm or a drought, but it can help people recover when those things happen. It's like a safety net – there to catch people if they fall."

Anil flutters up to join us. "The soil feels happy and healthy," she says.

"Justdiggit are heroes at restoring the land," I say, "bringing shade back to dry places, and empowering communities to bring land and life back into balance."

Caroline nods. "Everyone working together," We follow her gaze to a group of farmers working nearby. They are smiling and focused, raking, digging, planting, and tending the land with care.

A tall woman with silver-streaked hair welcomes a visitor in a long-sleeved shirt and a wide brimmed safari hat, downing tools and shaking him by the hand. "The help we received to take out insurance gave us peace of mind," she says. "After the flood, it meant we could plant again. It gave us the start we needed."

"We were pleased to be there for you," the man smiles. "The real heroes are the ones who work the land and keep going."

I turn to Caroline. "He's right. But how can we help?"

"By planting seeds of ideas," she says. "Like Lydia did on the night before the dinner, ready to grow into something marvellous to help others."

"It's why we're here," I say. "The Lady had a dream to cool the planet, to buy time to change the way people live. We left it up to Lydia and used the dream she planted in Emmanuel to support The Lady's aims as well. But The Lady developed it further to involve children as the key to a better future."

"So how come you are in Kenya, all of a sudden?"

"We met the founders of Justdiggit in The Netherlands. They wanted us to see the grass grown from the bunds used for animal grazing, and the grass seed collected and sold by the women in the community as a new livelihood. We learnt that regreening has led to increased rainfall and improved air quality."

"Even before that, the Winds of Change insisted on bringing us here," Anil adds. "They shared a dream with us about the desert and the arid lands of Africa. It led to The Lady supporting Justdiggit, Communities EverGreening Africa and the CEGA project we'll visit this afternoon."

"Aha," says Caroline. "I've heard that the Thika Road Christian School is performing a play written by The Lady, which will help fund their projects."

"Yes. It's another reason for being here," I smile. "Queen Titania sent The Lady a dream about our Nature Summit at the Temple of the Four Winds and the storm they stirred up in protest around it. The Lady used her imagination and wrote it down."

"She also made a silent promise," Anil adds, "to encourage schools around the world to protect lands like these, to help communities thrive."

Caroline gazes out across the grove. "People facing extreme weather deserve the security and stability to pull through, knowing they won't lose everything each time disaster strikes. That's what Humanity-Insured is all about – ensuring people can work through negative experiences to recover, building back with resilience, ready to reach new heights."

"We're heading off to see what the children are doing with Communities EverGreening Africa, so we'd better get going. We'll see you tomorrow."

"You'll be impressed," Caroline smiles.

Hearing the whispers of the soil beneath us and the hum of possibilities in the air, we wave Caroline goodbye and head for the hills.

***

Peeking through the leaves of an old ficus tree, Anil and I watch in amazement at the activity and purposeful energy of the children working in their garden below.

"Have you ever seen such determination?" I ask. "Look at those young ones, digging and planting as if their very future depends on it."

"There's something stirring in these schools," Anil replies. "They call it a 'greening initiative'."

I lean closer. "I know that, but not much more."

"I tuned in to the visionary behind this project."

"Shadrack, you mean?"

"Yes, he inspired the whole thing. These schools face so many challenges – crowded spaces, noisy streets, air so thick the children barely have room to breathe, let alone dream." Anil gestures towards a bustling group below. "And yet, look at them! They're transforming bare patches of land into nature havens, planting indigenous trees, growing food and flowers, basking in dappled sunlight as a new place to play."

"Shade and cool air attracts birds and bees," I say.

"And the school children are doing it themselves. They reuse what they have – even waste water gets a second chance, used to keep the gardens alive."

"What a way to learn," says Anil in awe.

"It's children using their creative magic," I reply. "Just look at those little saplings planted over there."

"That's the work of Kiang'ondu Primary School. They've grown over a hundred seedlings and shared five hundred more with other schools and local families. They're even protecting ancient trees like the one we're sitting in."

I run my hand along the bark of the ficus tree – rough, scaly, spongy, wrinkled with time, and wonder what stories it could tell after two hundred years of standing there.

"This feels like something the whole world should learn from," I say, "sparked by more schools ready to act and become a part of the story."

"Imagine students teaming up around the world," says Anil, "actively helping and showing their support, planting trees and swapping stories to help build a growing community of climate *doers*."

"Spreading the word like seeds. Even a light breeze will carry their stories further. The Winds of Change will be telling them at bedtime."

"And carry dreams with a sun-skip, hop and a jump, far and wide encouraging more little heroes like these," I say, noticing a small girl grinning in our direction. She waves.

"Flickeringfox!" I nudge Anil. "She's still young and heart-bright enough to see us."

We wave back, pirouetting through the air, doing handstands and cartwheels, giving a proper performance. The child laughs, and others gather to join in, puzzled at what's so funny.

"Joy can be contagious, even when we don't understand why," I say. "And the smallest idea can spread like wildfire."

Anil goes quiet for a moment. "Sky, do you ever wonder if The Lady could do more?" she asks softly. "She knows how to connect with people, but…"

"But what?" I prompt.

"I'm not exactly sure. It's just… if she wants those business leaders to help build a greener world, maybe she needs to speak a truth so clear that it stops them in their tracks."

"Defo," I nod, thinking hard. "Something bigger, like reminding them of how nature works."

"Yes, not by using control and commands, but through connection. Like a whole ecosystem where everything has its place."

I sigh. "Some leaders can't see things that way. They treat people like cogs in a machine – easy to replace and expected to obey, just like the Queen of Hearts once did. But the real magic happens when people begin to care."

Anil's eyes light up. "Look at what's happening here," she gestures towards the children tending their garden. "They're not just doing jobs; they're part of the story and growing with it."

"They plant a tree, and help it grow," I say. "What if work always felt like that? Meaningful, shared and alive with purpose."

"That's how it *should* feel," Anil says. "Not just clocking in for someone else's reward, but building something that truly matters together."

"Like tending a tree," I reply. "You care for it, and it gives back. That's how the world should work."

"No one here is shouting about money," Anil laughs, cupping a comical hand to her ear. "Just watering roots and growing hope."

I nod. "Imagine if grown-ups worked this way. With hands in the soil, minds in the moment, and hearts tuned to the future."

"Creating a beautiful garden," Anil smiles. "Everyone is different, and everyone is needed. Some shine in the sun, while others grow quietly in the shade. But all of them belong."

"The Lady's planting that kind of dream," I say. "Not just in school playgrounds, but in boardrooms too. And the children are lighting the path."

We watch a boy gently press a sapling into the ground, his fingers dusty with effort. "They remind us of something grown-ups have forgotten," I whisper. "That dignity doesn't come from power or money. It comes from being part of something alive, beautiful and balanced."

We sit quietly, letting the thought stretch between us.

"The world doesn't need shouting and fighting to change," I say. "It just needs a new story."

Anil grins. "And a few brave children to tell it." She hugs her knees, rocking back and forth as she gazes at the horizon. "The Queen of Hearts once forgot how to dream. All her shouting was just a way to cover up how lost she felt. But now…"

"…She's found a new way," I finish. "She walks among us in the material world, with Queen Titania's blessing, cheering on students and helping them find the light that shines from within."

"She still thunders, but now her storms have purpose," Anil adds. "She speaks for the children whose lands are drying and whose futures feel uncertain."

"The ones who used to fear her," I smile. "They're marching beside her now, with their teachers guiding the way."

"All it took," Anil says softly, "was one honest moment from The Lady - a truth, bold and clear, that awakened a hardened royal heart."

"Titania," I say, "sees courage when it shines."

"And the Murmurers?" Anil raises an eyebrow.

"Their tricks backfired," I grin. "Trying to spy on everyone only helped the Queen of Hearts see through the fog, dispelling those shadows of doubt."

We watch a girl gently winding a vine around a bamboo frame, her fingers patient and sure, growing hope for the future.

"Children know what to do," I say. "They share, they grow with a sense of what is right."

"The Lady believes this way of working can spread," Anil adds. "Like a ripple from a single stone, it can travel further than we think."

We sit in the stillness, watching the treetops sway in the wind. Anil breaks the silence.

"You know, Sky, I've been thinking about Shadrack. How he started with just a few trees and a deep belief in the land, and now there are whole communities learning from him."

I nod, smiling. "He planted more than trees. He planted purpose. Peter and Dennis too – the way they work side by side with students, not just teaching them but learning with them. It's inspiring."

I lean back and sigh. "Then there's Robert Gerlach and Klim, helping farmers find better ways – connecting them to funding that doesn't just demand more, but supports them to care for the earth."

"And in the Netherlands," Anil adds, "Katja, Simon, Sacha and Wytze – the young food forest farmers. These stories planted as dreams will sprout more of them, and more Shadracks, more Peters, more Dennises and more Roberts to rise."

"Maybe that's what we're dong here – helping write the next chapter. Not just for fairy tales, but for real life," I say. "Because magic happens when many hands work together. Suddenly, things that once seemed too big begin to seem possible."

Sweet fragrances waft through the air, the garden alive with gentle activity. It hums with quiet industry - laughter, birdsong, and the soft rustle of leaves.

"Anil," I say slowly, "what if at the next dinner, The Lady invites farmers to sit beside policymakers? What if companies that sell food really listened to the people who grow it, and supermarkets engage with them to discuss how they can make things work?"

"Caring about outcomes, not just profits," Anil nods. "Do you remember our first idea as a team? Changing the way supermarkets operate by rewarding those who choose plastic-free packaging?"

"Yes, and Kobalos's idea - giving away an acorn for children to plant. They would grow saplings and deliver them to local nurseries, collected by foresters to plant them on common land."

We picture it together, just as we did back then – when the West Wind saved us to the branches of an old yew tree during the storm.

"Now The Lady is giving children a voice, linking them together from different walks of life, uniting nations through shared school activities," Anil says, gazing upward into the clouds. "I didn't quite understand what she was doing at first. But I think I do now."

The sun dips westwards, casting golden light across the landscape. As evening gathers, I feel it - something powerful beginning to stir. Not in one place, but in many.

A new way of living, caring, and standing bravely for what is right is emerging. Quietly, across continents, in classrooms scattered around the world, children are rising to the challenge. Teachers who once worked alone are finding one another, sharing their stories, their questions, and their boldest hopes. Ideas stretch across oceans, travelling like seeds on the wind, cross-pollinating imagination with action. They are no longer waiting for change to arrive - they are actively growing it, together.

Beside me, Anil smiles, listening into my thoughts.

"It's happening, Sky. And it's only just beginning."

I spring to my feet. "Come on, Anil, it's time. We've seen what we came for - now we mustn't miss the performance!"

A breath of wind stirs the trees, and for a moment, the leaves seem to rustle with applause for something invisible and real. Embraced by the Winds of Change, Anil and I rise into the air - messengers, planters of dreams, carried forward by purpose and possibility.

Far below us, classrooms hum with the quiet miracle of children learning - and daring to believe in something better.

Hand in hand, we race towards a future that is already beginning to blossom beyond the trees – and is just within our reach.

THE END

EPILOGUE

A Word from The Lady

If you're holding this book in your hands, or listening to it in a classroom, beneath a tree, or in the quiet of your room, then you are already part of the story.

The magic we need now doesn't come from wands or wishes. It exists in compost bins and rainwater tanks, in raised voices at morning assemblies, in the quiet resolve of children planting trees or writing letters to those in power.

The magic lives in you.

The DCCI School Awards aren't here to orchestrate every next step or force the message. Our hope is simply to support schools and young people across the world by helping communities through the fundraising initiatives described in this story, and by uniting nations through a shared love of nature.

From Kenya to the coasts of Cornwall, from bustling Belgium to the mountains of Bhutan, children are reminding us of what many forget – that age is no barrier to courage, and that care and creativity are worth more than gold or glory.

Our awards are not just about recognition for outstanding talent. They focus on connection -

- between schools, - between generations,

- between the dreams of children and the wisdom of elders,

- between artworks, performances, fundraising presentations, and storytelling, where we celebrate excellence together.

We will restore what has been damaged. We will reimagine homes designed with the wellbeing of people and our planet in mind, rather than just profit. These homes will belong to future generations, not as monuments of consumption, but as sanctuaries of connection, intention, and renewal.

We will stop taking copper, sand, fossil fuels, and rare minerals hidden in the belly of Mother Earth - tearing into her crust to satisfy a hunger that cannot last. We will grow food that regenerates and heals the land, and tell stories that rekindle hope, kindness, purpose, and action.

Saving the natural world will not be the work of heroes alone; it needs all of us – leaders and listeners, the bold and the steady, the dreamers and the doers. It doesn't matter if you loud or quiet, standing in front or tending quietly behind. What matters is that we remain true to ourselves because every voice, every heart, and every hand counts.

I invite children to raise their voices, share their talents, and remind us that change begins with a single, simple choice: to care. You are not too small to make a difference. And we are not too late – we are right on time.

— *The Lady*

CREDITS

If you think you can do it alone, you are not thinking big enough. - **Wouter Crul**

Inspiration and a direct quote in Liam's story of Queen Titania's rule with the Queen of Hearts: *The Master and His Emissary* by **Dr Iain McGilchrist**.

Inspiration and direct quotes in The Lady's speech referencing the greatest environmental threats: **James Gustave Speth**, American Environmental Lawyer and former Administrator of the United Nations Development Programme; Co-founder of the Natural Resources Defense Council.

SPRITE SPEAK.

Clear-sky – true, undeniable, obvious.

Crisis averted: ironic formal way to express relief.

Defo – definitely

Flickeringfireflies! – playful exclamation of wonder, or sudden inspiration.

Flickeringfox! - playful exclamation of surprise or delight, exaggerated in the plural.

Fogkeepers - masters of doubt and distraction

Glow-lost – dimmed by worry or sadness

Glowgrow – when a good idea refuses to stay small or a magical moment of inspiration.

Heart-bright – full of joy

Moonblink – provocation.

Petalbright – beautiful or radiant.

Rizz - charisma or charm, often when impressed by someone.

Slayed it – overcame the challenge.

Shook - exclamation of shocked surprise.

Sun-skip – a day

UNCW: Under No Circumstances Whatsoever

Wingheavy – tired or overwhelmed.

Wing and whirl – equivalent to 'let's go!' or 'here we go!"

Zilch – nothing, zero or none.

ABOUT THE AUTHOR

Fleur Rossdale, a British author, moved from a distinguished career in promoting British interior design to writing children's literature in 2020. Her work blends imagination with purpose, nurturing a love for nature among young readers while inspiring them to protect the environment, believe in themselves and unite across borders through shared ambitions. Her books are more than stories - they are calls to action, encouraging children to become compassionate changemakers who help communities around the world.

In support of this vision, Fleur founded the DCCI School Awards - a global initiative inviting schools to host their own climate action award ceremonies inspired by *The Woodland Sprite Series*. These in-school events celebrate achievements in Drama, Art, Music, Oration, and Fundraising Presentations, all rooted in themes and characters in the series. The DCCI School Awards is a growing movement of educators, artists, scientists, and environmentalists working together to empower the next generation of environmental leaders.

Alongside her close-knit team, Fleur partners with schools to raise money for real-world environmental projects featured in her third book, *The Farm*, bringing storytelling to life as a catalyst for change. These include pioneering regenerative agriculture initiatives in both Europe and Kenya. In a unique literary twist, the very projects described in the narrative are supported by the outcomes of the DCCI School Awards, creating a powerful and poetic surrealist connection between fiction and reality.

Award Winners are invited to an international DCCI School Awards ceremony, where they receive recognition for their achievements and gain the opportunity to network with global industry leaders, philanthropists, and impact investors. The event also serves as a platform for senior students to explore mentorships and internships, offering a bridge between youthful idealism and real-world leadership.

The first schools to bring Fleur's climate action play, *Taken by Storm*, to life on stage in Kenya are The Thika Road Christian School and the Millennium Global International School, both supporting Communities EverGreening Africa (CEGA) at the Awards ceremony to take place in November 2025. Fleur Rossdale's work represents a new model of storytelling, where books do not just entertain but awaken purpose, inspire action, and bring communities together to heal the Earth.

www.dcci.earth

ABOUT THE ILLUSTRATOR

Nuno Gomes Vieira, based in Rio de Janeiro, brings the Woodland Sprite Series to life with evocative illustrations. With a bachelor's degree in architecture and a passion for visual storytelling, his artwork deepens the emotional and imaginative reach of the series – bridging story and setting in ways that resonate with children across cultures. Nuno is passionate about creative storytelling through images, particularly in fantasy or science fiction and connects with the Woodland Sprite Series in protecting nature from harm.

Printed in Dunstable, United Kingdom

64175701R10111